SALES, SECRETS & SUSPECTS

A Dogwood Springs Cozy Mystery

SALLY BAYLESS

Paperback ISNB: 978-1-946034-24-3

Kimberlin Belle Publishing LLC

Contact: admin@kimberlinbelle.com

Publisher's Note: This is a work of fiction. Names, characters, places, and incidents are a product of the author's imagination. Locales and public names are sometimes used for atmospheric purposes. Any resemblance to actual people, living or dead, or to businesses, companies, events, institutions, or locales is completely coincidental.

Cover art by DLR Cover Designs, www.dlrcoverdesigns.com.

Chapter One

AT FIVE MINUTES PAST FIVE, I hitched my large black tote onto my shoulder, stepped into the hall, and locked my office. I hesitated a moment, running a hand over the sign on the door that said "Libby Ballard, Museum Director."

Then I headed down the ornately carved walnut main staircase of the Dogwood Springs History Museum with my footsteps echoing through the empty building.

Which, sadly, had been empty all day.

Before five, of course, Imani, the education coordinator, and Rodney, the curator, had been with me in the museum. But we hadn't recorded a single visitor for Thursday, August 3. Even though August was the height of vacation season, a prime tourist time.

At the base of the stairs, I made sure all the lights were off, then went outside and locked the front door of the museum, a big, white, two-story Greek Revival that had once been the home of a local businessman here in the Missouri Ozarks.

In contrast to the museum, and in spite of the sticky heat of early evening, the rest of downtown was hopping. Tourists wandered in and out of the quaint shops that lined both sides of Main Street and offered candy, gifts, jewelry, and accessories. Couples chatted in the shade under the maples that had been planted in openings in the sidewalk and admired the giant baskets of pink, purple, and white petunias that hung from each antique light post. And groups of people gathered by the Dogwood Springs Bakery, the casual Dogwood Café, and the upscale restaurants that dotted the street, perusing the menus posted outside while they waited for tables.

Dogwood Springs, known as the prettiest town in Missouri, was a tourist mecca. People came from all over the US to see the blue-green springs, the dogwood trees that filled the town with blossoms every April, and the hard maples that turned orange, red, and gold every October. Charming bed and breakfasts, an award-winning winery, and restaurants far above the normal small-town offerings had sprung up to cater to those tourists, as had the shops that lined Main Street.

I passed the bakery and inhaled deeply, detecting the sweet scent of brownies. There were so many things to love about this town.

When I moved here two months ago, I thought Dogwood Springs was the perfect place to start a new life after my divorce. After all, it wasn't just a place I picked at random. My mother had been raised here, and I had fond memories of visiting my grandparents here as a child. Plus—an added bonus to someone like me, who loved history—my great-great-grandmother had once been the mayor. She'd helped make Dogwood Springs what it was today and was still seen as a key figure in the town's history. So much so that a professor at the local university was writing her biography. I even owned the pearls she had once worn.

The town was a beautiful place, a good place, filled with kind people, and when I arrived, I'd firmly believed it was a place where I could rebound from disaster.

But it was proving to be harder than I'd thought.

Despite the throngs of tourists in town, the murder that had taken place at the museum on my first day of work had been a public relations nightmare. Thus far, my marketing efforts had been as effective as if I'd tried to walk past the bakery without going inside on a Wednesday, the day the owner made shortbread.

Thankfully, Rodney, Imani, and I had a plan to change things at the museum, a plan that began with me attending a local auction in two days. Even the effort we'd put into our strategy sessions made me feel more hopeful. Whatever the stressful situation, things were always better with a plan.

After a fifteen-minute walk, I arrived home at my apartment, the first floor of a plain, two-story house built in 1900. While some homes of that era were full of architectural details like wide baseboards and ornate crown molding, my apartment was far less elaborate.

After the hit my finances took with the divorce, I didn't

need elaborate. And at age thirty-two, I knew what I wanted —a place that was close to work, fell within my budget, and had character. My Elm Street apartment was perfect. The mantel was original, hand-carved, with initials I'd found hidden underneath that matched the first owner. An enormous maple in the yard made the concrete slab front porch a shaded oasis. I shared the house with Bella, my golden retriever, and Cleo, my best friend who lived upstairs.

I stepped into the entryway, unlocked my front door, and Bella immediately greeted me.

She trotted over from the front window, where she'd been watching for me, gave a single woof, and rubbed her head against my leg, a none-too-subtle hint that I should pet her.

I willingly obliged, and when I bent down to hug her, she licked my cheek.

"Oh, I'm glad to see you too, sweetie." Tension I hadn't realized I was carrying melted from my shoulders as I petted her head. I dumped my purse on the couch and followed Bella to the kitchen, where she headed to the back door, ready to go out into the small yard.

I let her out and sat on the concrete steps, happy in the sunshine in spite of the humidity, enjoying time with my beloved dog.

When I moved to Dogwood Springs, I had hoped to find a cat or a dog that needed a home. Instead, Bella, who had belonged to a retired FBI agent who had been the former tenant in my apartment before he passed away, had found me. When she'd needed a home, I'd adopted her, foolishly thinking I was doing it to help her. I'd quickly realized she gave much more to me than I could ever give to her. Bella was supersmart and full of love, and she made my whole life better.

A few minutes later, my upstairs neighbor and best friend, Cleo, drove into the gravel alley between our house and the one next door. She pulled her old red Jeep into the open bay on her side of the detached garage.

"Hey, Libby." Cleo waved and yanked down the garage door.

I waved back.

Cleo's short, blond hair glinted in the sun as she walked toward me. Even after a long day on her feet as the owner and most sought-after stylist at a local hair salon, her movements were energetic, her personality bubbling through. And somehow, she managed to look put together while wearing a simple outfit of skinny jeans and a vivid purple T-shirt. Maybe because she was taller and slimmer than me?

In contrast, I was average height, average weight, and wore my dark hair shoulder length, in what once had been a bob. At the end of the day, especially after walking home in the heat, I looked hot and rumpled. Thanks to a heavy level of ragweed pollen in the air today, my green eyes, which I normally considered my best feature, were itchy and a little bloodshot.

Bella ran over to greet Cleo, and Cleo scratched Bella's ears and told her she was more beautiful than any client she'd seen all day at her salon.

"How was the museum today?" Cleo took off her

prescription sunglasses and replaced them with her regular glasses. Her brown eyes softened. "Any more visitors?"

I stood. "No. Still pretty empty." Even with Cleo, I was embarrassed to say exactly how bad the numbers were. If I couldn't turn things around, we might not be housemates much longer.

"Surely, the museum board is understanding. You've had a rather unusual situation."

I tipped my head, acknowledging her point. The murder of my predecessor had been a shock to me and to peaceful Dogwood Springs. And it had definitely made my job running the non-profit harder. After the murder, the museum had been closed by the police for several days. "At first, when we reopened, numbers were great. But I'm afraid those may have been people who wanted to see where the murder took place, not visitors actually interested in history."

Cleo frowned. "That seems a little ghoulish."

"I agree, but at least they paid the entrance fee." Even if they may have found me—the person who couldn't help but stick her nose in to catch the killer—more interesting than the exhibits. I let out a sigh. It wasn't simply about filling the museum's coffers. People needed to visit so they could see how fascinating and important history was. "But when school opens in a couple of weeks, Imani and I have lots of tours lined up." Not a real moneymaker, as we cut school groups a big discount, but at least the museum wouldn't be so empty. "And we've got a fabulous plan to get the town excited about history again."

"Oh, what's the plan?"

"September 16th is the official date the town was founded, back in 1845, when it was called Silersville. We're hosting a town birthday party, with cake and games and prizes and a new display about the town founder." At more than one hundred and fifty years old, the town deserved a party.

Cleo nodded. "That does sound good. I'd come to that, even if we weren't friends."

"Excellent. We think if we can get locals, like the bed and breakfast owners, excited about the new exhibit, it should lead to more tourists coming in. We're reaching out to them especially. After the murder at the museum, I've got a pretty good idea we're not the first tourist spot people have been recommending."

"Do you have flyers about the party? I could give them to my clients."

"We do. And that would be wonderful. Thank you, Cleo."

If all went as planned, the birthday party would turn things around. After the big event, we had several months of in-house programs planned, as well as community outreach.

"Happy to help. Is there anything else I can do?"

"If I didn't know you work every Saturday, I'd invite you to go to an auction with me."

"Ooh, how fun. I love auctions."

"I hope it's fun. Rodney's having his knee replacement surgery tomorrow, so I'm in charge of attending the auction of Marjorie Billington's estate and buying an armoire that belonged to Jedidiah Siler."

"The town's founder?"

"Yep. I wish you could go. I could use the moral support."

Cleo raised her eyebrows at me.

"I've been to auctions before, even bought a few things, but Rodney's afraid that if people see me bidding, they'll think the armoire is a valuable antique—which it really isn't—and bid the price way up, beyond what the museum can afford. I think his nervousness has rubbed off."

"Who's running the auction?" Cleo pulled a half-drunk bottle of Diet Dr. Pepper out of her purse and took a swig.

"Wilson Sales."

"Then you, my friend, are in luck. Not only am I the best hairstylist in town—who you should really let give you a trim—but I've also got connections."

A tingle of hope bubbled up in my chest. "You know someone at Wilson Sales?"

"My cousin Sheila has worked there for years. Is there a preview tomorrow?"

"There is."

"Let's go after I get off work, and I'll introduce you."

"That would be fabulous. Thank you."

Knowing someone at the auction, feeling like I was more on an even footing with the locals, who all seemed to have known each other since grade school, would be wonderful.

I'd really lucked into the perfect spot when I rented my

apartment. Not only had I found Bella, but Cleo had welcomed me right away and, in just two short months, become the best friend I'd had in years.

And with her help, hopefully, I could buy the armoire for the museum and make the town's birthday party a big hit.

The days without visitors would fade to a distant memory, and the museum would once again be a success.

Chapter Two

THE NEXT DAY WAS FRIDAY, and I was determined to start the day with a good attitude. I put on my favorite green shirt, the one that matched my eyes, and dressed up the outfit with my pearls.

Attendance at the museum did improve that day. Slightly. One woman came in during the afternoon. But Imani and I took full advantage of the time we had to work out more details for the birthday party. We made huge progress, and the day sped by.

That night, Cleo suggested we go out for Mexican, my favorite, before the auction preview. I suspected her idea stemmed from a desire to cheer me up, but I didn't argue. Wasn't everyone happier with a basket of hot tortilla chips and some queso and salsa?

After dinner, I drove us back toward downtown, passing Grove University, which formed the southern edge of Dogwood Springs.

I tried to keep my eyes firmly on the road but couldn't help taking a quick glance toward the computer science building, a glance I hoped Cleo wouldn't notice.

No such luck.

I'd barely looked back at the road before she spoke. "Has he called?"

"No." I pressed my lips together. "And it's probably for the best."

"Really? The most eligible bachelor in town talks about taking you out and then disappears off the face of the earth, and that's a good thing?"

"He didn't disappear. He just didn't call. And really, I'm in no place to start dating, anyway."

Cleo sniffed. "It's been eight months since your divorce and two years since you and your husband separated. You're in the perfect place to start dating."

I shook my head and gestured in front of the car at a group of college students who may have started their weekend at noon and were weaving their way across the street. I'd far rather have Cleo think I was focused on my driving than talk about Sam Collins.

I'd met Sam shortly after I moved to town. He'd made a fortune in tech in California, then sold his company and taken a job teaching computer science at the university. I briefly considered him a suspect in the murder of the former director of the museum but quickly cleared his name. After that, we'd had some great conversations, discussing a mysterious, valuable painting by a notable American artist named Clayton Smithton. Sam had found the painting in the historic home he bought outside of town, a home that had coincidentally once belonged to my family.

For a time, I'd been excited at the thought of going out with him. But when he didn't call... Well, it didn't do a lot for my already bruised ego or my lack of trust in men. No matter what Cleo said, I didn't need more of that negative energy in my life.

I navigated around another group of college students and headed for the Billington house.

According to Cleo, Marjorie Billington had died of cancer a couple of months back. Her house was a few blocks from downtown on a street that, after World War I, had been the most exclusive address in town. Even amid its lovely neighbors, the huge, French revival house stood out, sitting on a yard that took up a full block. The home had been lovingly maintained and had perfectly manicured grass and plantings that looked like they were put in by a landscape designer. Cleo said the house had belonged to Marjorie's husband's family.

Based on the glare I got from an older woman as I searched for parking, I'd say that Marjorie's former neighbors only barely tolerated the noise and fuss of all the people at the preview. I'd been to enough auctions to imagine they were going to be even less happy tomorrow.

I parked my eight-year-old Camry on the street and approached the house, feeling a bit like the hired help.

Cleo, on the other hand, was in her element, waving to half the people we passed and whispering little tidbits about the others. Before I met Cleo, I'd always heard that hairdressers know every secret in town but thought it was an exaggeration. It wasn't.

An enormous tent, suitable for a wedding party, had been set up on the side lawn of the house. "I called Sheila last night to tell her we were coming. She said they don't rent a tent like that for every auction," Cleo said. "But Danny Larsen, one of Marjorie's two great-nephews, wants his half of the proceeds from the sale like yesterday. So they don't want to reschedule, even though there's a strong possibility of rain." She pointed to a group of people outside the front door. "There's Sheila."

We walked up the curving stone path to the front door, but before we went in, Cleo ran over to hug the woman she'd indicated. "Sheila, this is my friend, Libby Ballard, the new director of the history museum." Cleo turned slightly. "Libby, this is my second cousin Sheila Dillon."

We said hello, and Sheila called over a guy who looked like he was in high school. She told him to remind every person going in that the sale would start promptly at nine, not a minute before. Then she led us into the house and turned to me. "Are you interested in anything in particular?"

"An armoire, eighteenth century," I said quietly. "But I don't want to draw attention to it."

Sheila gave me a wink and tucked her shoulder-length blond curls behind her ears. "Let me show you those *dishes*," she said, placing heavy emphasis on the word I hoped would throw other shoppers off the scent. "I think they'd be a lovely addition to the museum." I followed her up the stairs to the bedrooms, wondering if I was the only one who thought Sheila dressed like a country music star. She looked to be about forty-five and wore big earrings, a red plaid shirt with pearl snaps, and a jean jacket decorated with a large American flag made of sequins on the back.

After showing me some attractive and rather rare milk glass, a writing desk that Marjorie Billington believed had been used by a former governor, and a collection of fairly common political buttons from the 1950s and '60s, she waited until the stripped-down bedroom was empty of other shoppers and led me in to see the armoire.

If I hadn't known the history of the piece, I might not have looked twice. The armoire was about seven feet tall, probably maple, and had a Palladian cornice. It stood on tapered cone feet and had a carved scalloped skirt and two doors, one of which was covered with a spotty mirror. All in all, it was a rather poor rendition of Hepplewhite style in rather bad condition. According to Rodney's extensive research, though, this piece had been the prized possession of Jedidiah Siler. Or, more likely, the prized possession of his wife, Frances. If Jedidiah was typical of most male settlers of the time, his prized possession had probably been a horse. Or, since we were in Missouri, maybe a mule.

I looked the piece over, opening the doors and pulling out the two small drawers to check the dovetailing. After making sure no one was in the hall, I used the flashlight app on my phone, lay on the floor, and peeked underneath but found no markings. I pulled the armoire away from the wall, and, attached to the back with three tacks, I found a small piece of paper that Rodney would consider gold.

A man named Tobias Brown, who identified himself as a woodworker living near Dogwood Springs, had used a manual typewriter to document on an index card, now yellowed with age, that in 1963 he repaired the left-hand drawer. He explained the provenance of the piece, stating that Jedidiah's then elderly son Ethan had told him personally that his father hauled the armoire here by covered wagon when he and his wife moved from New York to Missouri in 1845.

Goosebumps sprang up on my arms. Dogwood Springs, which was then called Silersville, was founded in 1845!

I pointed out the card to Cleo, one finger against my lips. Since I'd moved to Dogwood Springs, Cleo had become a dear, dear friend. She did, however, have a tendency to be a bit loud.

She peeked at the card, and her eyes widened. She gave a silent nod.

I snapped a photo of the documentation with my phone and scooted the armoire back against the wall.

"Have you seen enough?" Sheila's tone was blasé, but her eyes twinkled.

"I have. Could we go out in the yard and chat?"

"Sounds good to me." Sheila led Cleo and me out beyond the crowd on the back patio to an isolated spot under a big oak tree. Once we were well out of earshot, she turned to me. "You want it for the museum, don't you?"

"As an antique, it's nothing special. Old, but not a great

piece to start with. A little banged up. And to my taste"—I shrugged—"kind of ugly. But it should definitely be in the Dogwood Springs History Museum. The historical value of a piece brought west by the founder of the town is priceless."

"I tried to tell Danny, one of the two brothers who are heirs, that they should donate the piece to the museum, that the tax write-off was probably more than what he'd get at the auction, but he didn't believe me. He's the executor, and his younger brother lives out of state and goes along with everything Danny says." She rolled her eyes. "Marjorie had collected some very nice pieces. But despite what my boss has told him repeatedly, Danny's sure that this auction is going to be something comparable with Sotheby's. Frankly, I think the guy's been watching too much *Antiques Roadshow*."

I wasn't sure it was possible to watch too much of my favorite show, but I got her point. "Do you think I'll have much competition bidding for the armoire?"

Sheila leaned back on her heels, crossed her arms over her chest, and gave me a long look. "I don't want to do anything unfair, but Cleo told me that you're only here because of Rodney's surgery. And I know if he was here, he'd recognize all the players."

"He did tell me to watch for one woman who might be interested, Lynne Dunn. He said she's short and has long, snow-white hair."

"Lynne won't be here. I saw her at an auction a couple

of weeks ago, and she said she was going out west on vacation."

A tingle of excitement shot through me. I might be able to get the armoire for even less than I'd hoped. "What perfect timing!"

Sheila's lips thinned. "There's this other woman, though, who I think might bid against you. She asked a lot of questions about the piece."

"Who is she?" Cleo stepped closer to her cousin. "And why do you think she wants it?"

Sheila raised both hands, palms up, in front of her. "All I know is what she looks like. She's probably in her late fifties, has short, dark brown hair, and carries a leopard-print purse."

"Odd." And disappointing. I wanted to get that armoire for the museum. "It's not a great piece of furniture, but people collect all sorts of things."

"They do, which is part of what keeps Wilson Sales in business." Sheila angled her head toward the house. "And speaking of business, I should get back to work."

Cleo gave Sheila another hug, and I thanked her and told her I'd see her in the morning.

I'd also be on the lookout for the woman with the leopard-print purse. Hopefully, that purse didn't hold a lot of cash.

Now that I'd seen the documentation from Tobias Brown, I wanted the armoire more than ever. With luck, I could acquire it, and, once Rodney recovered from his knee replacement, he could add it to our upcoming display about the town's founder.

The display could debut at the birthday party event. The party would be a hit, allowing us to promote all our upcoming programs. And visitors would start coming to learn about local history, not simply to gawk at the place where someone had been murdered. Attendance would rise, and donations would roll in.

It might be a rather ugly armoire, but it was the first step in getting the museum back on track.

Chapter Three

ON SATURDAY MORNING, I got up extra early. I fixed a big mug of my favorite tea, a nice, strong blend from Yorkshire, England, and ate some toaster waffles while doing a crossword. Then I took Bella for a walk on Elm Street, admiring the flowers in all the yards as my neighborhood woke up.

Cleo, Bella, and I lived on the 400 block, where some of the places were rentals. As the house numbers rose, the percentage of rentals dwindled, and the homes grew fancier. But even on our block, the lawns were tidy, and every house had at least one spot of colorful flowers. The entire street—despite being named Elm—was lined with big, shady maples. Birds twittered in the trees, kids zipped by on their bikes, and two women watered their flowers. Both stepped out on the sidewalk to say hello to me and give Bella a pat.

Thanks to Bella's popularity, over the past several weeks, I'd met many of my neighbors, and I'd been encouraged to literally stop and smell the flowers as one gardener after another bragged about their roses. Truly, without Bella in my life, I'd probably have never met so many people and never walked in any direction except toward downtown.

That morning, we took our regular route, down Elm to Thirteenth, where we turned and came back. It was a path Bella must have taken many times with her previous owner. She always preferred it, only accepting variation when I suggested a longer route, turning at Eighteenth.

There was a small incident when she felt compelled to strain at her leash and warn the neighborhood about a squirrel with some rather loud barking, but I finally got her to calm down. I had come to understand that she considered this her personal mission. Some of my neighbors, though, were probably more concerned with getting a little extra sleep on a Saturday morning than with the shenanigans of what seemed to me to be a harmless furry creature.

After Bella and I returned home, I took a quick shower and pulled on a T-shirt, a short tan skirt, and tennis shoes. Then I packed some lunch and a water bottle in my big purse, put on sunscreen, making sure to get it especially thick on the back of my neck, and tossed a fold-up lawn chair in the back of my Camry.

I left a ten-dollar bill on the kitchen table, along with a note thanking Zeke, Cleo's teenage nephew, for stopping by to let Bella out at lunch. Even in the shade, today was going to be off-the-charts hot and humid. Bella would probably be fine out in the yard, but I felt better leaving her inside, and I knew she'd get a big dose of attention from Zeke.

The downtown area was still quiet at seven thirty on a Saturday morning. Oh, the Dogwood Café looked busy as I drove by, with almost all the outside tables full. But most of the tourists were still in bed or enjoying breakfast at the B & Bs, and any college students in town for the summer were certainly still sleeping.

Or slightly hungover and moving slowly.

As for me, I had a mission. The thought of outbidding the woman with the leopard-print purse and sending a text to Rodney to let him know that the museum had acquired the armoire filled me with energy. I'd been on the job for two months now, but far too much of my time had been taken up dealing with the aftereffects of the murder. At last, I was getting into the real work of running the museum.

When I left my apartment, I'd thought I'd be one of the first to arrive at the auction, but by the time I neared the area, people were parked on both sides of the street four blocks away. I squeezed into a spot and started walking toward the house, with my folding chair slung over my shoulder.

I passed a man pulling a preschooler in a wagon, a couple arguing about where they would store more dishes if they bought them, and the same woman who'd glared at me the night before, still in her driveway, still annoyed.

The event gave the neighborhood a carnival atmosphere, complete with a food truck selling cinnamon buns and drinks and a sign promising hot dogs for lunch. Still full of waffles, I avoided the cinnamon buns, although the smell was intoxicating and the temptation strong. Other people who'd brought lawn chairs had arranged them in rows under the tent, facing a large platform, apparently where the auctioneer would stand. From snippets of conversation I heard, most people planned to make a day of it. The auction house must have anticipated this, as a trio of pale-blue porta-potties had been set up on the east side of the huge lawn.

I added my chair to the last row and wandered through the crowd, looking for Sheila.

I spotted the kid she'd left in charge of the door last night but didn't see Sheila. For all I knew, though, she might be hauling equipment over from the auction house.

I went over to a folding table at one end of the tent to get registered.

"Welcome." A plump woman with curly red hair handed me a numbered paddle and a listing of the items for sale. "I'm Jeannie Wilson." She tapped the logo of the auction house on her navy polo. "One of the owners of the auction house."

"Nice to meet you."

"We're bringing stuff out bit by bit, because of the possibility of rain," she said. "If you want to see anything, go right on in the house."

I thanked her and scanned the listing. Aha! There was my quarry. Lot number 93, "antique armoire, door with mirror, two small interior drawers."

Lot 7 also caught my eye. "Three boxes of miscellaneous old clothing, condition varied."

Auction listings like that always filled me with a wisp of

fantasy that I might buy a lot for a pittance and open the boxes to find piles of historic clothing. After all, my first attraction to history had been the Smithsonian's display of the first ladies' dresses.

I decided to allow myself twenty dollars of my own money to bid on Lot 7. Most likely, the three boxes would be filled with stained, worn, kids' clothes from twenty years ago. After all, someone like Sheila would have recognized historic clothing and described the lot with verbiage that would draw higher bids. The dream of finding a treasure, though, filled the air. How could I not be infected? If I bought junk, I'd pitch it. If I found a treasure, I'd sell it to the museum at what I paid.

The loudspeaker squawked with feedback, and a big, bald man wearing a navy polo like Jeannie's cleared his throat into the microphone. "Take your seats, ladies and gentlemen. I'm Carl Wilson, and this here party's about to get started."

A buzz ran through the crowd, and I hitched up my purse and headed to my seat. People laughed and chatted, some boasting about outbidding each other, but the minute the bald man approached the microphone again, the crowd went silent.

He welcomed us, made sure people knew where to register for a number to use in bidding, and gave a leisurely spiel about the "exciting, valuable, chance-of-a-lifetime" items that would be sold today. Then he plunged in, talking a mile a minute, auctioning off Lot 1, four cardboard boxes filled with "surprises" as he termed it.

I kept my numbered paddle firmly under my left thigh. I'd bought a box of "surprises" at an auction before, and they turned out to be sticky old plastic flowers. I liked taking a chance, but not that much of a chance. I was here for Lot 93, and if the spirit moved me, I might bid on Lot 7.

While the auctioneer coaxed the bid on Lot 1 up to $13, I surveyed the crowd. Three rows ahead of me, off to my left, I spotted a leopard-print purse on the grass next to the chair of a woman with dark hair. Perfect. I couldn't see her face, but I could keep an eye on her and try to determine what type of bidding strategy she used. For the moment, though, she appeared to be reading the listing of items to be sold.

Ten minutes later, the auctioneer popped open the lid on one of the boxes of Lot 7 and pulled out a hideous pair of men's golf pants. "Any of you gentlemen would look mighty snazzy in these!" He held the waist wide, showing that the pants had to be at least a waist size 52. "And you can't say they won't fit. I think these could be altered to work for anyone in the audience."

The crowd roared.

"How about we start the bidding at five dollars?"

A woman sitting at the end of my row raised her paddle.

She looked at least ten years younger than me, twenty-one or twenty-two, and if I had to guess, based on her orange-and-green patterned dress, which screamed 1960s, I'd have said she was hoping for vintage clothes in those boxes. But how high was she willing to bid?

Vintage Girl and I jockeyed back and forth, each raising the bid by a dollar. I tried to judge by her expression how far she was willing to go, but she kept her eyes on the auctioneer.

When she bid nineteen dollars, though, she looked over at me. And her expression wasn't encouraging. It was the bored, almost defiant face of someone who could bid all day to get what she wanted.

"Thirty dollars," I called out. Yeah, I knew I'd set a $20 limit for myself. I knew my financial situation after the divorce wasn't exactly what a financial planner would call ideal. I knew those boxes might be full of nothing but golf pants. But sometimes my stubborn streak gets the best of me.

And you know what? It worked.

Vintage Girl blinked at me and shook her head when the auctioneer tried to get her to bid $35.

Lot 7, three boxes of miscellaneous old clothing, condition varied, was mine.

I got up and looked again for Sheila, eager to share the news of my victory over Vintage Girl, but still didn't see her.

Then, unable to resist, I slipped into the house and headed up the stairs toward the bedrooms. Lot 93 wouldn't come up for hours. I could take one more peek at the armoire.

I reached the door of the second bedroom on the left and casually glanced inside. A plump, dark-haired woman stood near the armoire. Her mouth was pulled up tight, and her eyebrows, which looked over-plucked and penciled in, were drawn together. From her elbow hung a leopard-print purse.

"Oh, I didn't see you." She stepped back from the armoire and gestured toward it. "Rather ugly, isn't it?" She was interested. I could tell. This wasn't my first rodeo.

I tried to act as if I'd never noticed the piece before. "I'd have to agree with you. Not a good example of Hepplewhite style."

I feigned interest in a chest of drawers, and she left the room.

I listened carefully, waiting until her footsteps receded.

Then I practically leapt across the room and looked over the armoire once more.

The best part of the whole piece was the documentation by Tobias Brown that was attached to the back. I was about to edge the armoire away from the wall to make sure the paper was still there when I realized I'd never looked closely at the repair work the man had done. I moved back to the front of the piece and pulled open the door.

Sheila's body tumbled out, landing on my feet.

Chapter Four

I SCREAMED AND STUMBLED BACKWARD, running into the chest of drawers. For half a second, I stood there, one hand propped behind me on the top of the chest, the other spread wide over my pounding heart.

Sheila no longer wore the red plaid shirt or the sequined jean jacket, but she still had the country music star style going, with a hot pink western shirt, a denim skirt, and sandals with hot pink sequins. Her blond curls, though, were mussed, and dried blood covered a wound on her temple.

"Are you okay?" The young guy who Sheila had left in charge of the front door last night charged into the room, then froze. He looked at Sheila, then at me, then at Sheila again. "Is she... Is she dead?"

"I think so." I stepped closer and placed two trembling fingers on the side of Sheila's neck.

After a futile attempt to find her pulse, I held my hand under her nose.

No breath came out.

My chest tightened, and I looked up. "I'm afraid she's gone."

He paled.

He was a big guy with dirty blond hair and the muscles of a linebacker. Probably great part-time help for a moving company. And probably a guy who considered himself an adult. Right now, though, he looked like a scared little kid, a kid who might pass out.

I felt somewhat shaky myself. Slightly out of phase, as if the situation were surreal. But if I fell apart, I thought he would as well. So, I tried to act strong.

"Can you call 911?" I asked. Perhaps he'd do better with something to focus on other than the body.

He pulled a phone from his back pocket and tapped the screen quickly.

The two of us hurried into the hall, where we huddled, close to the door to the room, nervously scanning the hall but unwilling to leave Sheila's body.

Soon he was talking to the police. He moved the phone away from his ear and put it on speaker. "I'm supposed to stay on the line until someone gets here." He glanced toward the room with Sheila's body and shuddered. "Man."

I nodded. "I know." It was horrible. She'd been so full of life last night. "I only met Sheila briefly, but she seemed really nice."

"She was nice. She helped me get hired, and she was fun

to work with and…" He blinked and looked away. After a moment, he looked back at me. "I'm Josh. Josh Bradford."

"Libby Ballard."

His nose wrinkled. "Ballard. Aren't you the woman who found the dead body at the museum?"

"Yeah, I am."

His mouth tensed, and he took a step toward the doorway, as if guarding Sheila's body.

I held up both hands, palms up. "I didn't kill her. If I did, would I have opened the doors to the armoire and let her body fall on me?"

Josh's face grew even paler.

"What's going on here?" Detective John Harper strode down the hall toward us.

And he didn't look happy to see me.

Detective Harper, who I'd met earlier in the summer, must have been at the auction given how quickly he'd arrived upstairs.

He was a short, heavyset man with a salt-and-pepper buzz cut, dark eyebrows, and a presence that said he'd seen about everything life had to throw at him.

Despite his scowl, I felt a whole lot better with him around.

He quickly examined the body, then told Josh and me to come outside with him. He stopped the auction, told everyone to stay in the yard, under the tent, and—as soon as other members of the police arrived—allowed most people to leave after they gave one of the officers a name, address, and contact information.

For a few minutes, though, until other officers arrived, the scene was chaotic. I was pretty sure some people wandered into neighbors' yards and slipped away.

Still wobbly, I stood with my back against one of the tent poles and eyed the crowd, wondering if the killer was still among them.

I wasn't intentionally eavesdropping, but I couldn't miss the conversation between Jeannie Wilson and a man with a black mustache who looked to be about forty. "Have the police said how soon we can reschedule the auction?" His nasal voice was loud and easy to hear.

I couldn't make out her response, but from the expression on her face, I'd say Jeannie didn't want to be talking to him.

"Your husband said everything would be sold today," the man continued. "And that we'd have the money in less than two weeks. I expect you all to do everything in your power to meet that two-week deadline."

Ah. He must be Danny, the great-nephew so eager to get his hands on the money from Marjorie Billington's estate.

Jeannie said something else I couldn't hear, and the man stormed off and disappeared into the crowd under the tent.

After a pair of officers checked the house, they led Josh and me into what had been Marjorie Billington's living room, along with three other people: Jeannie and Carl

Wilson and the man with the black mustache, who introduced himself as Danny Larsen.

Detective Harper waved us toward the two large floral couches and left Officer Tate, who I'd also met earlier in the summer, to keep an eye on us. One by one, the detective was to interview the five of us, Jeannie Wilson first. She twisted her hands together as she followed Harper out of the room, her elbows tucked tightly against her torso as if they might hold in the fear that radiated from her.

Personally, although I still shuddered when I remembered Sheila's body falling on my feet, I wasn't afraid for my life. It had looked like someone bashed poor Sheila over the head. With four other people in the room, one of them Officer Tate, I didn't think anyone was going to attack me.

The question was whether one of these people might have killed Sheila.

Not Josh. He'd been as shocked as me to see the body and was still a bit pale. I gave him what I hoped was an encouraging smile.

And neither Carl nor Danny gave off an obvious I-just-committed-murder vibe. Before the officer told us to remain silent, Carl voiced concerns about the customers at the auction and the lots that had already been sold and were still under the tent. His comments all seemed reasonable to me, what I'd expect from the business responsible for the event.

Danny didn't say anything, but he didn't look guilty, just irritated. I'd guess a murder the day of the auction was the last thing he'd wanted if he hoped to get his inheritance quickly.

Detective Harper and Jeannie had only been gone a few minutes before she was sent outside to take inventory of the lots that had already been sold.

I was called in next. I followed a young officer I didn't know into the room that must have been Marjorie's library. Once, the space had probably been warm and welcoming, the walls lined with much-loved books. Now, with the book-shelves dismantled and grouped in one corner, the room seemed forlorn, too large for the furniture that remained, two matching rose-colored armchairs and a small round end table.

Detective Harper sat in one armchair and gestured to the other. The young officer stood by the door, notepad and pen in hand.

"It appears you've found another dead body, Miss Ballard."

I shifted in my seat. When we first met, I learned the detective had known my mom in high school and thought she was a pain. His initial opinion of me, if I had to guess, hadn't been much better. The last time we talked, though, when he'd learned I'd adopted Bella, he'd called me 'Libby' and sounded a lot more friendly.

He adjusted a notepad in his lap. "Can you tell me what happened?"

I explained that Cleo had introduced me to Sheila the previous evening and that I was attending the auction as part of my job, hoping to buy a piece of furniture that had belonged to the town founder, with the plan to display it at the museum. I'd gone to take one more look at the armoire, I said, talked briefly to the woman with the leopard-print purse, and after she left, opened the door to check the drawers. "And when I did, the body fell out."

He nodded and scribbled something on his pad.

"But last night, Sheila was wearing different clothes," I said. "An outfit that was red, white, and blue. So, I think she must have been killed this morning."

A look of pain passed over Harper's face. "Miss Ballard, I realize that some people feel compelled to get involved in a murder investigation when they find the body, out of some false sense of responsibility. But"—he shot me a pointed glare—"you need to stay out of this."

"I understand, but I really think you need to find the woman with the leopard-print purse. She was alone in the room before I came in, and she looked uneasy, maybe even guilty." I edged forward on my seat as the ideas spun in my head. "She could have killed Sheila and shoved her in the armoire right before I arrived. Her body was still warm."

His eyebrows drew together. "You're sounding far too excited about this. I appreciate the information, but that's where this stops. I do not want you playing detective. You do remember that with the last murder, you almost got yourself killed?"

I sank back in my chair. "I do." I certainly didn't want to be in a situation like that again.

"Is there anything else?"

I shook my head.

"Don't leave town, Miss Ballard. I may want to question you again. You may have seen something and not realized it at the time."

"Am I a suspect?"

"No. I just think you're too curious for your own good. Too nosy."

I winced. The very word my ex had used from time to time to describe me. Personally, I thought it was perfectly reasonable to want to understand things. The world needed to make sense.

I glared at Harper, scooped up my big black purse, and went out to look for my lawn chair.

Jeannie Wilson, who was back at the registration table, took my money and gave me a receipt for Lot 7. "You'll be able to pick up your items after the police go through them. They don't want anyone leaving with the murder weapon, unintentionally or on purpose." She glanced up at the expensive tent and let out a sigh. "The rest of the auction will be rescheduled."

I took the receipt, found my lawn chair, and folded it up. Then I hefted my purse onto one shoulder, the lawn chair onto the other, and walked toward my car.

What a horrible morning. I'd failed at my goal of buying the armoire. For all I knew, the auction might be postponed until after the event celebrating the town's founding.

And far more importantly, how was I going to tell Cleo that Sheila was dead?

∿

Despite its sunshade, a freebie from the local bank when I opened an account, my car was sweltering. I dug two clean tissues out of my purse, carefully folded them in half, and used them to protect my hands from the steering wheel, which had to be 150 degrees. I could, of course, sit for a minute, let the AC run, and wait for the steering wheel—and the rest of the car—to cool down. But I wanted to get away from the Billington home as fast as possible.

I took Main most of the way through downtown and jogged over a block to park behind the library. Then I walked into Cleo's salon and told the receptionist that I needed to speak with Cleo privately.

She answered the phone and held up one finger.

Fine. I could wait. I sank into one of the cushy upholstered chairs and soaked up the soothing ambiance of the salon with its restful shades of teal and gray, soft instrumental music, and the faint scent of lavender.

It was nice but not enough to get me to relax after what I'd seen.

A few seconds later, Cleo came into the lobby, her eyes red, her face puffy. She squeezed her eyes shut for a second and pressed a hand against her lips, then caught my arm and drew me into the room where she had her salon station.

I pulled her into a hug, and she began to cry.

"I'm so sorry." I patted her back. "There was nothing I could do."

She stepped back. "I can't believe she's gone. And that you ... found her." She made a vague gesture with her hands. "Jeannie Wilson knows my mom, and she called and told her what happened."

"I'm really sorry, Cleo. She seemed like such a fun person."

"She was. Sheila was one of my favorite people. She was the one adult I could be totally honest with when I was in high school, even when I did really stupid things. She was the person who encouraged me to go to New York when both my parents told me I was crazy. And now she's gone." Cleo broke down sobbing and turned to dig a tissue from her purse. "How can this be real?"

After she wiped her nose, she turned back to me. "And what if the police never find her killer?"

"I'm sure Detective Harper will solve the case." Despite his comment about me, he seemed to be doing all the right things. "Imani told me that his brother, the chief of police, is back on the job, so the detective doesn't have as much administrative stuff to do."

"Yeah, but the police are still short-staffed. And there have been all those burglaries. Practically every shop on Main Street has been hit." She glanced over at a small tower of shelves in the corner of the room, neatly lined with haircare products. "I guess I'm lucky no one wants to steal hairspray."

"Wow. I read in the local paper about two break-ins downtown, but they hadn't seemed like that big of a deal."

"I think they've tried to keep most of it out of the paper. You know, because of the tourists. But how can Detective Harper find Sheila's killer if he has to deal with a burglary every other day?" Cleo set her jaw and blew out a heavy breath.

"I had no idea it was so bad." If the police were too over-whelmed to find Sheila's killer, who would?

Cleo looked me in the eye. "You were so smart, Libby, figuring out who committed the murder at the museum."

I bit my lip. Smart might not be the best way to describe it. Detective Harper had been right. I had indeed nearly gotten myself killed. Plus, he'd specifically told me to stay out of this investigation. And the image of Sheila's dead body still hovered at the edge of my mind, probably waiting to fill my thoughts as soon as I was alone.

But it would be nice to show the detective that I wasn't simply nosy. I was good at solving puzzles—crosswords and other word games and murders in mystery novels. And Cleo was right. Whoever murdered Sheila needed to be put in jail.

I'd always been someone who believed that everyone should follow the rules. But with the way my ex had manip-ulated things after our divorce, I believed even more strongly that justice mattered.

Most importantly, Cleo was my best friend. How could I say no?

"Okay." I squared my shoulders. "I'll try. Or rather we'll try. I know Alice and Zeke will want to help, just like last time." Cleo's nephew and Alice VanMeter, the president of the museum's board of directors, had worked with Cleo and me to solve the murder at the museum.

Cleo let out a ragged breath. "They will. I know the four of us can figure this out. Thank you."

I took a step back. "The four of us? Do you really want to be involved? I'd think, since you were so close to Sheila…"

"I want to help." Cleo stood taller. "I have to do something."

"Okay." I pulled her into a sideways hug. "Then the four of us will figure out who did this."

Chapter Five

THE NEXT DAY, Cleo was with her parents all day, but we texted back and forth, including Alice and Zeke, and made plans for the evening.

In the morning, while it was still cool, Bella and I played a game of fetch in the backyard with her favorite tennis ball. I considered going to church, but by the time I thought about it, I should have already been showered and out the door. By eleven, it was steamy, so I worked on my regular weekend chores. I made a trip to the grocery store to stock up on essentials, like shortbread cookies. And—after a quick check for spiders, which gave me the creeps—I hauled my laundry to the machines in our unfinished basement.

An hour later, I dumped my whites and part of my clean colored clothes on the bed. I hung up a few things and went back down to get the rest of my colored clothes, some of which took longer to dry.

On earlier trips to the basement, I'd taken Bella with me, but this time, she was nibbling at a few leftover bits of kibble in her bowl, so I headed downstairs alone.

I came back upstairs to find her on my bed, burrowed into the warm laundry.

"Bella!"

She raised her head and angled it to one side. On her head, sitting like a beret, was one of my forest green washcloths.

I bit my lip to keep from giggling. "Down," I said in the sternest tone I could muster, and I pointed to the floor. I did not need dog hair all over my bath towels, but she looked so cute that it was hard to be mad.

And even harder when she instantly hopped to the floor, hung her head, then rubbed it against my leg.

"What am I going to do with you?" I rubbed her ears and reminded her that she was not supposed to be on the bed, especially not in the middle of my clean laundry.

Honestly, it was a good thing that her former owner, Don Felding, had trained her. Except for things related to her health, I was a pushover.

All in all, though, we had a nice Sunday. I was home almost all day, and Bella loved it. I had a feeling that if she had her way, I'd give up the whole museum gig and stay home all the time.

After dinner, I brushed her coat until it gleamed, clipped on her leash, and stepped into the entryway that led to my front door and the stairs to Cleo's apartment.

I leaned up the stairwell. "Ready?"

I heard a clunk from inside Cleo's apartment, and then she emerged. "Sorry. I just got home from my parents'. My mom's thinking about hosting a reception after the memorial service so people can reminisce about good times with Sheila."

"That sounds really nice." I held the door for Cleo and Bella. "I bet people have lots of fond memories of her."

"I know I do," Cleo said quietly.

Bella, who seemed to have a sixth sense about when people were hurting, walked over and rested her head against Cleo's leg.

Cleo patted Bella between the ears and turned toward downtown.

The three of us walked to the Dogwood Café. Cleo was understandably subdued and, except for making an occasional comment to point out a particularly lovely yard, I remained silent. Cleo was more of an extrovert than I was, but in times of grief, I thought it was more important to be present than to spout platitudes. So, I walked along, enjoying the evening. The sun had dipped below the trees, and the heat of the day had passed.

At seven, the downtown area was still full of tourists and, thanks to the candy shop, scented with the faint smell of fudge. The shops were open until eight, the fine-dining restaurants were packed, and it was probably only because the café closed at eight that one of the green metal tables in the outside dining area was empty.

Cleo went over to snag it while I made my way more slowly, allowing Bella to stop at three tables to be petted.

Maybe, if I lived in Dogwood Springs for five years, I'd have as many friends as Bella. She and her previous owner must have spent hundreds of hours taking walks through the town and making friends.

Eventually, Bella and I made our way to the table. She settled down in an out-of-the way spot, and I pulled a chew toy from my purse to keep her occupied.

The owner of the café, an older man named Marcus, waved to us. Even though I was still fairly new to town, I had already been adopted as a local. Marcus knew my name, knew Bella, and probably knew what I'd order.

"Cleo, Libby." Alice walked up to the table and hugged us both. "I was so sorry to hear about what happened, Cleo. Sheila was such a lovely person. And it had to be so shocking for you, Libby."

Alice was one of those people who made everyone around her more comfortable. She volunteered at the museum every Monday, and I relied on her as much as either of the paid staff. Even with all that had happened earlier in the summer at the museum, I had never seen her flustered. She was always dressed in pants and a stylish polyester blouse, her tousled light-brown hair always looked perfect, and she always exuded calm. Maybe that calm came with being in your fifties, living somewhere all your life, and being married to a man whose gift basket business was so successful that you didn't need to work. Or maybe it was just Alice, and she'd been exactly the same when she was twenty.

Alice sat on the other side of Cleo and waved toward the

entrance to the outdoor dining area at a teenager with brown eyes just like Cleo's. He wore baggy shorts, black Converse tennis shoes, and a T-shirt that advertised what I thought was a band. "Over here, Zeke," Alice called.

Tall and skinny, Zeke easily wove his way through the tables toward us, then slumped into the remaining chair.

According to Cleo, Zeke had recently aced his driving test a week after he turned sixteen. Not surprising. His motor skills had probably been honed by years of gaming, and the kid was really smart. He'd been tech savvy enough to help me gather important clues when I solved the murder at the museum, so clever that Sam Collins had been impressed and wanted to talk to him about what he planned to study in college.

But Cleo said Zeke had been too intimidated by Sam's reputation to follow up. And I was in no place to ask Sam to reach out.

Zeke petted Bella, redid the band around his long, dark ponytail, and looked across the table at Cleo.

"Sorry, buddy," Cleo said.

"Yeah. It's just ... wrong, you know?"

"Believe me, I know." Cleo's lips tightened. "It makes me furious that someone did this."

Zeke gave Cleo a look of sympathy, then pulled a dessert menu from where they were wedged between the napkin holder and the salt-and-pepper shakers. Food was a high priority for him.

Our server appeared, took our drink orders, and told us

that the fruit cup was locally grown peaches and raspberries.

"That's what I'm having," Alice said.

Cleo and I picked up dessert menus and, after a bit of debate, I made a choice.

The server returned with coffee for Cleo and Alice, an enormous cherry soda for Zeke, and iced tea for me. She took our orders and hurried inside.

As soon as she walked away, Cleo leaned in. "Thank you all for coming. The more I thought about all the burglaries in town, the more I wanted us to try to figure out who killed Sheila. The police have got too much going on to make her murder the top priority."

Alice took a sip of her coffee. "I know the police are going to do their best, but I don't think Dogwood Springs has ever had this much serious crime at one time." She rolled her eyes. "At least not since I moved here."

I glanced over at her. "I thought you were from Dogwood Springs."

"No. My husband is. I grew up in Westfield, about half an hour from here. I met him when he opened his first grocery store there."

I held up a hand to stop her. "Grocery store? I thought he ran a gift basket business."

"He does, but it started out as baskets with food products from the store, and I worked in the bakery, decorating cakes. We moved here when our oldest was four because the schools were better."

"Oh." Clearly, I still had a lot to learn about my new friends. But I needed to focus on the investigation.

I looked around the table. To an outsider, Alice and Zeke might have seemed like odd additions to our sleuthing team. Alice, respectable and proper, old enough to be my mom. And Zeke, only sixteen and probably more comfortable with people his own age. But they'd welcomed me to town, we'd already solved one mystery together, and I knew I could count on them. And those differences among us, like the differences between family members, were part of what made us a good team.

I drew in a deep breath. "Okay, then, let's get started. I've got our first suspect. There was a woman Sheila had told me was interested in the armoire on Friday night. She was in the bedroom, looking at the armoire, when I arrived yesterday. And she seemed stressed, maybe because she'd just committed murder. But I don't have any idea who she is."

"What did she look like?" Zeke picked up his soda, plunged the straw deeper a couple of times to stir up the pool of cherry syrup gleaming red in the bottom, and looked at me intently.

"She had a leopard-print purse, and she was about my height, plump, with dark brown hair."

"Straight? Curly? How was it cut?" Cleo asked quickly.

"Uh, sort of wavy. I think you'd call it a chin-length bob?" Cleo might know all the hair terminology, but I didn't.

"Did you speak with her?" Alice asked.

"Yes, but I didn't learn anything. I think we both were trying to convince the other not to bid on the armoire."

"That's a clue." Alice's eyes gleamed. "She had to have a reason to want that armoire. Did she have an accent?"

To me, having grown up in Columbus, Ohio, everyone in Dogwood Springs had a slight southern accent, and Alice's was the most pronounced of all. No need, though, to point that out. "She sounded like everyone else around here."

Cleo smiled at the server, who set a slice of coconut cream pie in front of her. "But Sheila didn't know her. So, this woman might be from Missouri, but she wasn't from Dogwood Springs."

The server gave Alice her fruit cup, Zeke a huge brownie sundae, and me a piece of lemon meringue pie.

I quickly took a bite and let out a soft moan. Absolutely fabulous. Delicate crust, extra-tart filling, and a perfectly browned meringue topping. Combined with my iced tea, it was a delicious dessert.

Zeke scooped up a large spoonful of ice cream and brownie. "Well, maybe Mr. or Mrs. Wilson will know who she is. Don't you have to register at an auction to get a number?"

The rest of us, our mouths full of dessert, made sounds of agreement.

"Then," he continued, "if we could see the list, we could narrow it down to women who aren't from Dogwood Springs. And Mr. Wilson or his wife might be able to rule out other women who come to lots of auctions because Sheila would have known them."

Cleo, Alice, and I looked at each other. Why hadn't we thought of that?

"That's my nephew." Cleo patted his shoulder. "I know my sister-in-law disagrees, but I think he gets all those brains from our side of the family."

Zeke looked over at her. "Really, you think I get it from Dad?" His eyes scrunched up, as if he wasn't sure that was a good thing. After all, from what Cleo said, Zeke and her brother were at loggerheads over where he'd go to college.

Cleo rolled her eyes. "For heaven's sake, don't tell him that. The genius gene was probably recessive." She tapped Zeke on the shoulder. "You got it. And, of course, I got it."

Alice chuckled. "This woman sounds like an excellent suspect, but there's a chance that she had nothing to do with the murder. I think we also need to consider Rick Dillon, Sheila's ex-husband. I heard that he's been back in town for about a month."

"Definitely." Cleo broke off a piece of pie crust with her fingers and nibbled on it. "Mom says he bought a house that's only a couple of blocks away from Marjorie Billington's place. And he was not at all happy ten years ago when Sheila wanted a divorce. He never hit her, but once, when she wasn't home, he got drunk, threw a plate at the wall, and then drove his car into a tree. Who knows? He could still have had feelings for her." She popped another bite of crust in her mouth.

"Ooh. He sounds like a good suspect. Maybe he wanted

to get back together, and she told him she wasn't interested. Maybe it got heated." I took a sip of iced tea.

Cleo held up one finger, as if she'd thought of something, then chewed quickly and swallowed. "The person who would know all the details about Rick would be Sheila's best friend Adelaide Murphy. Hold on." She pulled out her phone and called her mom.

The rest of us sat quietly, eating our desserts.

A few minutes later, Cleo hung up and blew out a frustrated breath. "My mom says Adelaide just left for one of those tech-free, total relaxation spa vacations. I got her number. I'll call later and leave her a message, but we probably won't hear back for days."

The four of us looked at each other.

"We've had roadblocks before. Let's keep thinking," I said.

"Let's say it was Rick. Why would he kill her at the auction?" Zeke asked.

"Well." Alice tapped her lip. "It does open up the list of possible suspects more than if he were to kill her in her home."

"And we don't know where Sheila was killed," I added quickly. "Only that her body was found at the auction."

Cleo's eyes clouded.

Maybe I should refrain from mentioning the body.

I cut off another bite of pie, careful to get exactly the right ratio of crust to filling to meringue. "Another thing we should consider is that the crime may have had something to do with the sale or the auction house." I'd thought Jeannie seemed nervous about having a murderer on the loose, but maybe she was nervous because she was the killer. Or because she knew her husband was.

Cleo nodded. "So, that means we have to consider Carl Wilson and his wife, Jeannie, and that young guy who was sitting in front of the house when we were there."

"Josh," I said. "Although he didn't act very suspicious. He seemed shocked to see the body."

"Josh Bradford," Zeke said. "He's not a murderer. His younger brother's a good friend of mine. But Josh would be a good person to ask about the Wilsons."

"That gives us four suspects." I counted them on my fingers as I named them. "Sheila's ex-husband, Rick. Carl Wilson. Jeannie Wilson. And the woman with the leopard-print purse."

Alice's nose wrinkled. "I can't really see Carl and Jeannie committing a murder at one of their auctions. If it was one of them, it would make more sense to kill Sheila somewhere else."

"Unless it wasn't planned," Zeke said. "One of them might have killed her in anger."

"True," Alice agreed slowly. "But they still wouldn't be at the top of my list. And we haven't located the woman with the leopard-print purse yet."

"Well, we certainly know how to find Rick." Cleo spread both hands palms down on the table. "He's got a job out at the nature center at Dogwood Springs Park."

"I think you should be careful around him," Alice said.

"We will, but I do think we should talk to him first." I glanced over at Cleo. "Would you feel up to going with me?"

"To figure out who killed Sheila?" Cleo sat up taller in her chair, her face grim. "You bet."

Chapter Six

ON MONDAY, Cleo had the day off, and we planned to begin our investigation over my lunch hour.

Since Imani and I were the only staff at the museum these days, we took turns covering the front desk. She was five months pregnant and earlier on had suffered horribly with morning sickness. Even though it had passed, she still ate breakfast late, at her desk. So, she had asked for the late shift, and I had a lunch break from twelve to one.

I mindlessly gobbled down my lunch at eleven-thirty while writing an email to a potential donor. Shortly before twelve, I hit send. I didn't really have time to start another task, so I tidied my office for a couple of minutes, straightening the papers on my desk, dusting the dark wooden window blinds, and giving some water to the daisies in the three blue carnival glass vases on my desk.

Cleaning complete, I looked around the room. The Dogwood Springs History Museum really was a beautiful place to work. My office had a high ceiling, creamy white walls, ornate crown moldings and baseboards, and a large mahogany desk. Plus, the whole building had a smell that made me happy, the smell of history—a mix of furniture polish and mothballs and slightly musty papers and books.

Right after twelve, Cleo texted from the parking lot behind the museum, ready to go talk to Rick.

I grabbed my purse and went out to meet her. After a quick stop at our house to let Bella out for a few minutes, we drove to Dogwood Springs Park, located east of town.

One nice thing about the area, which had taken me a while to get used to after living in Philadelphia, was how close everything was. Even though the park was outside the official city limits, it didn't take long to get there.

As I knew from the museum, the grist mill powered by the spring water had drawn early settlers to the area, but the town itself had been established slightly farther west, along a pioneer road that became a military highway during the Civil War and later Route 66 and was now Interstate 44.

We pulled into the parking lot and found a spot under a big oak near the nature center. Inside, the woman at the desk told us Rick was giving a tour. If we waited a few minutes, he should be done, and we could talk with him.

We went back outside, followed a paved path along the stream that flowed from the springs, past the old grist mill and a short, rocky waterfall, and up to the pool where the spring water emerged.

The large pool was a deep blue-green, and it was probably twenty feet across. In the center of the pool, there were two places, side by side, where the surface of the water rose slightly, as if twin hoses were pouring water from below. According to a large sign, scientists now knew that the water actually came from one springhead, but the stream of water was divided far below the surface by a lump of rock that was slowly being eaten away. Back when settlers reached the area, they had seen it as two springs and named it Dogwood Springs.

The air was still, but the gurgle of the water flowing over the waterfall was soft and soothing. A dragonfly hovered over the spring pool, and I spotted a tiny frog on one of the mossy rocks along the edge. Although the temperature was close to a hundred degrees and the humidity was stifling, the path was shaded by large oaks, and the air felt cooler near the spring. Probably because the spring water, according to the sign, was 56°F.

A group of six stood by the spring's edge, listening to a man in an olive uniform, who Cleo said was Rick. Like Sheila, he looked to be in his midforties. He was of average height and build, had thinning blond hair and a deep tan. He answered a question from a young teenage boy in the group, telling him that scuba diving was prohibited in the spring except by research permit.

The question seemed to be the last. The group followed the path toward the far side of the grist mill.

Rick turned and headed back toward us.

Cleo waved and introduced herself.

Rick's eyes narrowed, then lit. "I remember you from when you were little. You were a firecracker." He chuckled, but a half second later, his face fell. "Sheila loved you to bits."

Cleo's lips tightened. "She did."

I stuck my hand out, introduced myself, and explained that although my grandparents had lived in the area, I hadn't been out to the springs since I was a child. "Cleo was coming out today, and I tagged along. I remembered really liking it here."

"It's a special place. That spring produces eighty-five million gallons of water a day." Pride rang in Rick's voice. He turned to Cleo and spoke more softly. "I'm really sorry about Sheila. I still can't believe she's gone."

"That's actually why I'm here," Cleo said. "Mom wanted me to let you know that a few weeks from now, there will be a memorial service and a reception afterward. We know you two divorced a long time ago, but..."

I silently cheered. Cleo was shifting the conversation exactly as we'd planned. "Such a horrible thing," I added.

Rick's face softened. "I appreciate that, Cleo. Please tell your mom I'll be there, and keep me posted once you decide the date. I—" He glanced away, then turned back toward us. "I don't see any reason not to tell you. I guess at forty-seven, I finally grew up and realized what was important in life. One of the reasons I moved back to Dogwood Springs was that I was hoping to get back together with Sheila."

Cleo's eyes widened. "You were? Had you talked to her?"

"I had. She was supposed to go out to dinner with me this Friday night." He rubbed the back of his neck. "I guess that won't be happening." His gaze fell. "And I feel like it's my fault."

Cleo and I looked at each other and then back at Rick.

"Your fault?" I tried to keep my tone sympathetic, but every nerve in my body was on alert.

"I'd been trying, every day for the past week or so, to take her a little present to let her know how much she meant to me. Nothing big, you know, but a flower I picked or a muffin from that bakery downtown." He looked at us, as if waiting for us to tell him that his plan had been sure to win Sheila's heart.

Cleo and I nodded.

"I knew Sheila. She was probably the best employee Carl and Jeannie Wilson had ever had, working late every night and early the next morning. The morning she was killed, I stopped at the donut shop by the university and got a chocolate cake donut with chocolate frosting. I drove to the Billington house real early and knocked on the front door. She opened it but said she was running from one thing to the next, so I just handed her the bag and smiled. The last time I saw her, and I didn't even talk to her." He shook his head.

"That seems like a nice thing to do," I said. "I don't see how that makes her death your fault."

"Not that," Rick said. "What happened later. As she ran off, she called out and said I could walk around a bit to see what all they had for sale at the auction. I was in the living room, looking at a TV, when I heard her arguing with some guy. I hadn't seen anything I wanted to buy and had decided to head home. I walked right past the room where she and that guy were, and I didn't do anything to help her. I mean, Sheila was pretty independent, and I didn't think she'd take too well to me implying that she couldn't take care of herself, but what if that guy killed her?"

Cleo leaned in closer. "Do you know who it was? And did you tell the police?"

"I did tell the police, but I don't know the guy's name. He was tall, maybe six foot two, with a big black mustache. No beard, just the mustache."

"Danny Larsen," Cleo said.

"That's it. The police officer recognized him from the description too. Apparently, he's one of Miss Marjorie's heirs."

"One of two great-nephews," I said. "Did you hear what they were arguing about?"

Rick twisted his mouth to one side. "No, just that Sheila sounded annoyed. It may have been nothing, but I still feel like I should have done something."

"If Danny's the killer, he's the one who needs to feel guilty, not you." Cleo patted Rick's arm. "I think what you did makes sense. I don't see Sheila being happy if you got involved. She wasn't the kind of woman who wanted a hero. She wanted to take care of herself."

"Yeah, but what if this time she couldn't?" Rick's lips thinned into a line.

"Even if Danny was the killer, you had no way of knowing he'd murder her," I said.

He gave a wry grin, as if he didn't really believe me, and

looked at Cleo. "I appreciate the invitation to the memorial service. I'll be there." He turned and walked toward the nature center, head down.

"Wow." I looked at Cleo. "Do you think he's right? That Danny Larsen killed her, and Rick could have prevented it?"

"I don't know." Cleo let out a long sigh and headed toward the car.

I walked slowly, trying to put the clues together. "I can't imagine why Danny would have wanted to kill Sheila. Her work with the auction was helping the estate get settled, helping him get his inheritance. Would their paths have crossed outside the auction?"

"Not that I know of," Cleo said as we climbed in her Jeep.

"Maybe she caught him stealing something from the estate, like a piece of jewelry or a valuable coin." I could picture someone slipping a small item into their pocket. "Then he'd get all the value and not have to split it with his brother."

Cleo paused with her seatbelt pulled halfway across her chest. "Danny's a jeweler. He owns the shop on Main Street. So he would know a good piece of jewelry if he saw it."

"If it was a really expensive piece of jewelry, it might be a good motive." I gave the park one last look as we drove away. Even away from the spring pool, it was a beautiful area, with acres of grass, pavilions with groups of tables, and an occasional lone picnic table under a shade tree.

Cleo clicked her seatbelt and started the car. "It doesn't make sense. Why steal something when the auction was about to start? If I planned to steal something, I'd do it when fewer people were around."

"Yeah, you're right. But maybe he didn't see the item until the last minute." I found the website for the jewelry store on my phone and opened it. "You know, the jewelry store is open until eight tonight. I could wander in on my way home from work and have my pearls checked to make sure the clasp is still in good condition." How fortunate that I'd worn them again today.

"And say what? 'Did you kill Sheila? And would you like to murder me next?'" Cleo asked in a high voice. "I know I asked you to try to solve this, but now I'm thinking that was a mistake. I already lost my favorite cousin. I don't want to lose my new best friend."

"I won't say that." I shot her a look of frustration. "I'll think of some smart thing to say."

Cleo glanced over at me again. "You promise?"

"I promise."

Her face relaxed, and she nodded.

Now I just had to figure out what that smart thing was.

Chapter Seven

AT THE END of the workday on Monday, I grabbed my purse and headed to the jewelry store.

From the outside, the store looked like many other shops on Main Street. Windows shining, attractive displays, and an awning—in this case a vivid purple—to protect tourists if it rained. Inside, though, it seemed far more elegant and refined than the candy shop or the accessory store or the bookstore. The walls were stark white, except for one that was solid black, matching the black velvet in the display cases. The air-conditioning, which had to be on high, was silent, and classical music, possibly Bach, played softly.

An older woman sat on a black leather stool, trying on ring after ring ... a large sapphire, a starburst of rubies, a huge square-cut emerald.

With each new piece, Danny told her the size of the center stone, and they discussed how it looked on her hand.

Finally, after Danny offered a ring with a large amethyst surrounded by diamonds, the woman shook her head. "I guess not today, love. I'll pop in next week and see if you get any new stock in."

"I'll be looking forward to it, ma'am. Always a pleasure. It's not every woman who can wear fine jewelry with such panache." He ran his thumb and forefinger down his mustache, as if he perhaps thought it gave him his own panache.

The woman beamed and left the store, her head held high.

Danny walked over to me. "Hello again. Can I help you?"

I unhooked my pearls and held them toward him. "I wanted to get these checked to make sure the clasp is still good. It's kind of delicate."

"Very smart," he said, taking them. "Let's go over where the light is better."

"Those rings that woman was trying on looked so nice. I —" Good grief. What was I going to say now? That I recognized her worn white tennis shoes as the store brand of a discount store? That her clothes were out of date and extremely worn? That I was surprised she could afford huge sapphires and emeralds?

"She has very good taste. One of my favorite customers. A neighbor when I was a child. She comes in every week, and we've been looking for years for just the right piece for her to add to her collection." I realized that he knew, and must have known all along, that she could never afford such jewelry. And yet he played along, allowing her the fantasy of fine jewels, and she probably left the store every week, the way she did today, walking tall and proud.

He held my pearls under a bright light, and almost immediately, his brow furrowed. "It's a good thing you brought these in." He pointed out places where the knots were frayed. "The clasp could use a little work, and these need to be restrung. They're lovely pearls, and this clasp looks antique. A family piece?"

"Yes." Although we'd sort of met after the murder, I introduced myself, explaining that I was the new director of the local history museum and the great-great-granddaughter of Elsie Dorsett, who had been mayor of the town in the 1920s and 1930s.

"Were these Elsie's pearls?" Danny looked down at them once more.

"They were."

"Then it's even more important that you get them taken care of."

We discussed the price and how long the process would take, then he slid the pearls in a small brown envelope, sealed it, added it to a file drawer, and gave me a receipt. "And I should officially introduce myself as well," he said. "I'm Danny Larsen, the owner here. I was at the auction because Marjorie Billington was my great-aunt."

"Then you have a connection to the history of the town, too. I attended the auction on behalf of the museum, hoping to buy the armoire that belonged to Jedidiah Siler."

Danny nodded. "Rodney Grant had talked with me about that piece."

"He just had knee surgery and sent me in his place to try to buy it." I gave a half shrug. "I guess it won't be for sale anytime soon. What a horrible thing to happen. Did you know the woman who died?"

"I did. We actually had a bit of an argument earlier that morning, which I guess someone overheard and told the police about. They were in here about an hour ago, asking me more questions."

I tried to look surprised, instead of impressed by the police. "Was the auction house not doing a good job?"

"No, nothing like that." His lips pinched. "And it wasn't what they thought—that I'd killed her." He huffed out a breath. "Why would I kill her? That auction had been planned for weeks. The last thing I wanted was for it to be canceled."

I tipped my head in acknowledgment.

"The truth of the matter," he said as he leaned forward, one elbow on the counter, "is we were arguing because I asked her out, and I guess I came on a little too strong."

"Oh." Was every guy in town interested in dating Sheila?

"Anyway, as I told the cops, I didn't kill her. I knew she'd come around in time. Some women just play hard to get." He gave an unctuous smile that made my skin crawl.

And some men didn't understand the word "no." Danny might have been kind to his former neighbor, but he was a jerk. There were a lot of jerks in the world, though, and being one didn't make Danny a murderer. The bottom line was that he had wanted the auction to take place, and I was ready to leave. I took a half step back toward the door.

"Anyway, I told them who they really should be investigating," Danny said.

I stopped walking. "Oh, who?"

"Sandy Byers." He angled his head to the right. "The woman who owns the gift shop a block that way."

"You think she killed Sheila?"

"All I know is that I heard Sheila talking with her boss, Carl. Apparently, Sandy was really mad at Sheila about something related to the auction house. And I saw Sandy at the auction that morning. You know what they say on the cop shows on TV—means, motive, and opportunity. Sandy definitely had motive and opportunity, and as for means, well, anyone can sneak up behind somebody and whack them over the head."

The image of Sheila's body flashed through my mind, and I shivered. "I guess so." I opened the door, more than ready to get away from Danny and his misguided ideas about dating.

A group of women walked through the open door with their arms laden with shopping bags. One of them waved at Danny.

His eyes lit up. "I've got some new bracelets you'll love," he said to her.

He promised to call when my pearls were ready, and I said a quick goodbye.

~

The next day at work, it felt like every time I hung up the phone, someone else called. Some of those calls were promising, with hints of potential donations and civic groups interested in me presenting a program about the museum, but they didn't leave me much mental space for murder suspects.

At the end of the day, though, I walked home, let Bella out in the backyard for a few minutes, and packed up a sandwich for myself and dinner for Bella. Then the two of us headed out of town toward the springs.

We came to a stoplight, and I turned to Bella. "I've got a surprise for you, girl."

She thumped her tail on the seat.

The light turned green.

A block later, I looked over at her. "Oh my gosh, Bella, yesterday Danny said that Sandy could have whacked Sheila over the head. Do you think everyone knows that's how Sheila was killed? Or does he know because he killed her?"

Bella looked at me with her tongue hanging out one side of her mouth but didn't reply. For a dog that was so smart, she didn't offer quite as much insight as I'd like.

I drove on, pondering my own question, and finally decided that, with how fast gossip spread in Dogwood Springs, the way Sheila had been killed was probably common knowledge.

But it was interesting, though, that if I believed Rick and Danny, Sheila had two men eager to go out with her.

It didn't make sense to be jealous of a dead woman, but, in a weird way, I was. How many times had my ex told me he loved me and said I was something special? Hundreds? Thousands? Then he'd cheated on me and replaced me with a woman eight years younger. Not a recipe for making me feel special. Or for building my trust in the opposite sex.

In fact, after my divorce, I promised myself that I'd avoid men. I weakened when I met Sam, but look how well that had turned out. He said he would call when the painting came back from the restorers. That had been more than six weeks ago, and I hadn't heard a word from him. And for a fairly small painting, restoration should only take two or three weeks. Of course, the restorer might have had other projects to finish first. And the work could have been more complicated than I thought.

But with the way Sam had smiled at me, I really expected to hear from him before the painting was done.

Instead, nothing. Which left me feeling even worse than before I'd met him. One more rejection in a—

Bella nudged my arm with her nose and gazed at me with love.

"You know what, girl, you're right. Enough already. I can focus on the disappointments in my life, or I can focus on the good things." If and when Sam Collins ever called, I wanted the museum to get the painting, but that was all. Other works by Clayton Smithton had sold for around a quarter of a million dollars, so it would be a huge coup if the museum acquired it.

Bella gave a soft woof.

"Yes, you are definitely a good thing," I said.

And she was. Everyone would be happier if they had a

pet, whether it was a parakeet or a tabby cat or an eighty-pound golden retriever.

I turned on the radio, switched it from news to the oldies station, and, as soon as they began playing Jackson Browne, turned it up and sang along.

Before long, I pulled into the parking lot by the nature center and went around to open Bella's door.

She hopped out of the car and wriggled in a circle around me, her tail wagging.

We ate our dinner at a picnic table under an enormous old oak tree. Kibble and canned food for her, like the vet recommended, and a turkey sandwich, an apple, and some chips for me. Water from a reusable steel bottle for both of us. Then I brought out my surprise for Bella, a Frisbee I'd bought the previous weekend.

My first few attempts with the Frisbee fell about three feet in front of me.

Bella retrieved them but looked at me as if she hoped I could do better.

It took a bit of warming up before my Frisbee skills returned. I probably hadn't thrown one in fifteen years. Finally, I got better, sending the Frisbee flying, and Bella caught it every time.

I didn't know whether she and her former owner had played Frisbee or if she simply had natural talent. Either way, she loved the game, leaping up to catch the flying disk and bounding back to me to drop it, covered in drool, at my feet.

At last, I told her we needed to head home. One of my

throws had gone a bit wild, ending in a patch that wasn't mowed where she ran into burrs.

Her fur needed a good brushing, and I needed to talk with Cleo about Sandy Byers. Somehow, we needed to learn what Sheila had done that made Sandy so angry.

Chapter Eight
____

ON WEDNESDAY MORNING, I was late to work.

After we got back from the springs the previous evening, Bella went crazy, barking at the fireplace like a whole army of squirrels had taken up residence.

She completely ignored the word "no" and the word "quiet," both of which I knew she understood.

It took hours and repeated promises that I would call the landlord and have him check the chimney to get her to calm down, and in the process, I forgot to set my alarm. I woke up so late that I didn't even have time to drink my tea, just fixed it in a travel mug and raced out the door.

I hurried up the stairs to my office at ten after nine, scrambling to unlock the door with the phone inside ringing.

I missed the call but called back as soon as I'd listened to the message.

A couple of weeks ago, I'd dropped off information about the museum with the director of the local community center, which provided childcare for ages five through twelve during the summer.

The call was from the director. The community center had made plans for the day to take all forty kids on a field trip to an outdoor water park an hour away. Right as they were about to load the bus, the director had gotten a call from her husband, who had heard on the radio that the park had been shut down for health violations.

The director was desperate. She'd promised the kids a surprise, a really fun surprise, and told them to bring their swimsuits. She could set up sprinklers in the yard at the community center at the end of the day, but was there any way we could offer an entertaining day for the kids?

Could we? Would Imani freak out if I agreed without asking her?

No, like me, she'd be thrilled that someone—anyone— was visiting the museum.

"Give us an hour," I said. I asked the age breakdown for the kids, made sure they were fine with eating their packed lunches on the grass in the front yard, and got off the phone.

The minute I hung up, I grabbed my tea—caffeine would be essential—and raced to Imani's office.

Imani was in her late twenties, at least three inches taller than me, and even at five months pregnant, still fairly slim. She had her box braids pulled up into a ponytail today and was wearing a darling olive-green maternity dress.

Given how much she talked about her baby and the way the dress fit, I'd guess she was wearing it more because she was excited about her pregnancy than because of a need for a larger waistband.

When I first met her, she had seemed quiet. Maybe that had been because of the murder at the museum, maybe because of issues she'd had with the previous director. Once I got to know her better, I learned two things: first, that her amazing eyelashes were, in fact, 100 percent real, and second, how fun she was. She was one of those people with an infectious giggle, and the two of us and Rodney spent a lot of time laughing during our meetings.

As I expected, she was delighted to have visitors back in the museum. We brainstormed, pulled marbles and jump ropes out of the storage room in the attic, and even found audio recordings on our phones so we could teach the kids how to square dance in the parking lot behind the museum.

The community center staff helped, but Imani and I did all the programming. I could tell, when we pulled out the supplies, that the kids thought marbles and jump ropes would be boring. But children didn't always have TVs and smartphones and extracurricular activities after school. Once upon a time, kids had to make do with what they had. Fun didn't begin with the semiconductor chip.

I knew dozens of jump rope games, Imani knew more marble games than I'd ever heard of, and the two of us, well, I don't mean to brag, but we taught those kids to do a mean do-si-do.

They had a blast.

When they left at four, I got two sodas from the fridge in the conference room and handed one to Imani. We collapsed onto chairs at the table.

Imani propped her feet on a chair. "Thank heaven I'm only having one baby."

I laughed.

For the next half hour, we just sat there, soaking up the air-conditioning, congratulating ourselves, and repeating all the great comments the staff and kids had made as they left.

I sent Imani home at four thirty and began tidying the museum, hoping for a second wind. It didn't come. I cleaned up the trash, wiped up a pool of splashed water by the sinks in one of the women's bathrooms, and stashed the box of jump ropes and the large bag of marbles under the desk in the main hall. Hauling them to the attic could wait for another day.

I trudged home, let Bella out, and stuck a frozen pizza in the oven.

Later that evening, when Cleo got home, Bella had another barking fit, as if trying to tell Cleo all about the squirrels. When I finally got her to be quiet, I called the landlord, left a message, and went to bed.

The next day, Cleo had a cancellation, which meant we could continue our investigation over lunch.

At five after twelve, Cleo pulled her Jeep into the parking lot behind the museum.

As I climbed in, she moved a bag of craft supplies to the back seat, and the two of us drove east of town about two miles. She found a spot in a gravel lot outside a large, red metal building with "Wilson Sales" painted on the side in big white script.

Hopefully, Carl or Jeannie would be there and could tell us if Danny's story about Sheila arguing with Sandy Byers was correct. Plus, as Zeke had suggested, they might have a name for the woman with the leopard-print purse. And, of course, we needed to see how they reacted to a discussion of Sheila's murder. Either one of them could be the killer.

"How do we approach this?" Cleo said, switching her prescription sunglasses for her regular glasses.

"Let's start by asking about the woman with the leopard-print purse." I opened my door. "We don't want to start with anything that might make them defensive."

"Good point." Cleo climbed out, and we walked across gravel with me wishing I'd worn different shoes. Cleo's tennis shoes, which she wore because she was on her feet all day cutting hair, were fine in the gravel. My ballet flats, not so much.

Inside, the space had concrete floors and was open all the way up to the high, metal rafters. One corner had been partitioned into office space. We went in through the office door and found Jeannie typing on a computer. She had a pen stuck behind one ear, peeking out of her red curls, and the empty dish from a frozen meal on the desk beside her.

"Hey, Jeannie." Cleo waved.

Jeannie looked up quickly. "Cleo, I didn't hear you come

in." She pulled the pen out of her hair, brushed a crumb off her shirt, and hurried over to us. "I'm so sorry about your cousin." She clasped Cleo's hands, and her eyes shone. "This place is just empty without her. I can't tell you how much Carl and I miss her."

Jeannie could be lying, I supposed, but she sure sounded sincere.

She turned to me. "And Libby, is it?"

I nodded. "Libby Ballard. I'm Cleo's neighbor."

"I hate that your first experience at one of our auctions was so horrible." Jeannie sighed. "What can I do for you all today?"

"So, we have a weird question for you." Cleo gestured to me.

"I saw someone I think the police should talk to about the murder," I said. "But to be honest, Detective Harper didn't seem that interested. I thought maybe if I could give him a name... The woman was in the room with the armoire right before I went in. But I don't know her name. And Sheila, well, Sheila didn't know her either."

I explained how Sheila had described the woman to me so I'd know who I might be bidding against, making it clear that she didn't do anything unfair to the other bidder. Somehow, even though Sheila was dead, I didn't want to get her in trouble with her boss. "The woman had dark hair, looked to be in her fifties, and had a leopard-print purse."

"She probably wasn't from around here," Cleo added. "Or Sheila would have known her. We wondered if you had a list of all the people who got bidding paddles. If we find someone we don't know, it might be her."

Jeannie's eyes lit, and she pulled a spiral-bound notebook from under a counter, opened it, and laid it on her desk facing us.

Cleo ran her finger down the names, stopping every now and then to confer with Jeannie about a name that seemed vaguely familiar. Between the two of them, they ruled out all but five names as people who lived in or around Dogwood Springs. Two of the five were men. One was a woman who came to lots of auctions, who Jeannie said Sheila would have known by name. And one was a woman with an unusual name who Jeannie remembered as being well past retirement age. That left one woman, Lisa Brown.

Jeannie jabbed a finger at the name. "She has to be the woman with the leopard-print purse!"

"Excellent." I pulled out my phone. "Do you mind if I take down her phone number and address?"

Jeannie turned away and whistled.

I made a note of the information. "Now we're making progress."

"Hey," Cleo said. "Was anything stolen the day of the murder?"

"Maybe something small, like would fit in your pocket?" I added.

Jeannie shook her head. "Actually, no. Carl and I were worried about that, what with all the confusion, but we don't think so."

"Bummer," Cleo said. "I mean, it's good that nothing was stolen, but that might give a reason for the murder and maybe another suspect."

"You know..." Jeannie looked around, as if she was afraid someone else might have come into the office without her hearing. "I have my own theory about who might have killed Sheila. I told Detective Harper, but I couldn't really tell if he thought it was worth following up on."

"Who?" Cleo and I said in unison.

Jeannie chuckled. "So, you have to promise not to say a word. Not a word!"

"I promise," I said quickly, and Cleo elaborately used her pointer finger to draw a cross over her heart.

Jeannie motioned for us to follow her into a small meeting room. The three of us sat in folding chairs around a metal table, and we all leaned in.

"Last week, we started sorting and listing items for an auction that comes up in a few weeks," Jeannie said. "The estate of Charles Byers."

Byers. That was Sandy's last name.

Cleo nodded eagerly.

Jeannie lowered her voice and angled her head toward me. "Byers was a judge here in town for decades. He retired maybe ten years ago, but he and his wife were definitely part of the Dogwood Springs elite."

I raised my eyebrows. "I didn't know there was a Dogwood Springs elite." Talk about big fish in a small pond.

"Of course there is." Jeannie pointed at Cleo. "Her family, for sure."

"Libby, your aunt and uncle were part of the same group," Cleo said. "You know, people who belong to the country club and have lived in town for generations."

"Being local is a big part of it," Jeannie said. "There's a bit of the town and gown divide here. I wouldn't ever consider someone affiliated with the university as part of the real elite, unless they'd lived here for decades and really gotten involved." She laid one hand on the table. "Anyway, Charles died recently, and his daughter, Sandy, hired us to auction off everything she didn't want."

I shot a look at Cleo. Ah, Sandy was Charles's daughter.

"When Sheila and I were going through Charles's library, we found a stash of antique photos of scantily clad women. Really, by today's standards, it was pretty tame. Lots of women hiding behind fans or well-positioned scarves. I mean, you see more skin exposed at the local pool. But Sheila found notes that indicated they belonged to Charles's grandfather, who was also a judge. She was all excited because, really, there's quite a market for that stuff, and she thought Sandy would be thrilled."

"Let me guess," Cleo said. "Sandy wasn't thrilled?"

"Not at all. In fact, she was angry because she thought Sheila had told people in town." Jeannie raised her hair off her collar, then let it fall. "Carl and Sheila both assured her that she hadn't said a word, but I wasn't sure Sandy believed it. Sheila could be a little ... chatty."

"Chatty?" Cleo let out a soft laugh. "Sheila was a gossip,

pure and simple. If she knew dirt on the family of snooty old Charles Byers, she wouldn't have been able to keep quiet for long."

"That's what I thought when you found her body," Jeannie said. "Sandy might have killed her to silence her."

"This sounds like a great lead," I said. "Detective Harper didn't seem interested?"

Jeannie shifted her weight, and the folding chair squeaked. "No. He really didn't. Which is frustrating. I want him to find Sheila's killer. It's—" She glanced at Cleo, then looked down and blushed. "Well, of course, the most important thing is justice for your family, but the murder is also bad for our business."

"I understand," Cleo said. "I'd be in big trouble if someone had been killed in my salon."

"Well." I looked at them. "Cleo and I can try to talk to Lisa Brown. And we can try to learn if Sandy Byers has an alibi."

"Really?" Jeannie sat back in her chair. "Oh, I remember now. You solved the murder that took place at the museum, didn't you?"

"I had help." I gestured to Cleo.

"Hopefully, we can solve this one." Cleo stood. "The killer needs to be caught."

"But we have to do it very carefully," I added. I picked up my purse, rose to my feet, and started toward the door, then turned back. "All three of us need to keep this quiet. We don't want one of us to become the next victim."

Jeannie shuddered and agreed. She followed us out and

asked Cleo to let her family know that she and Carl were thinking of them.

In my mind at least, she was off the suspect list.

Cleo thanked her, and she and I headed back to town, ready to take the next steps in our investigation, calling Lisa Brown and talking to Sandy Byers.

Chapter Nine

THE NEXT MORNING, I was wishing I kept snacks in my office when Alice called from her daughter's house, where she was watching her twin three-year-old grandsons.

"We were playing with Play-Doh, and I was making little flowers, and I had a wonderful idea!"

"Oh?" I saved the open file on my computer and sat back in my desk chair.

"I want to bake the cake for the town birthday party."

"But we're hoping to have two hundred people there."

"Not a problem. I'll start baking sheet cakes and freezing them. When we talked about the cake decorating I used to do, it got me thinking. I know why I left the job at the bakery, but I don't know why I stopped decorating cakes. I really enjoyed it. Not enough time after I had kids, I guess." She paused. "Of course, my cake won't be as good as one from the Dogwood Springs Bakery."

"Nonsense. I'm sure it will be delicious." I'd never eaten

a cake that Alice baked, but the woman did everything well. And frankly, the museum couldn't afford to buy cake for two hundred people from the bakery downtown. I'd been thinking of a cake from the grocery store. "It's a lot of work though. Are you sure?"

Alice laughed. "Haven't you realized, Libby, that I like to do things for this town? I've already been planning how to design it."

"Then I think it would be amazing." I thanked her profusely and hung up, picturing a photo in the newspaper of visitors happily eating cake. The town birthday party was going to be a fabulous event!

The rest of the morning flew by, and at noon, I ate the last bite of my tuna salad sandwich and my last carrot stick, drank some water, and headed home. After letting Bella go out in the backyard, filling her food bowl with lunch, and petting her for a few minutes, I walked back toward downtown.

In spite of my curiosity about Lisa Brown, Sandy seemed like a very good suspect, and my spirits buoyed as I neared the gift shop. If I found out anything that seemed questionable, I could tell Detective Harper, he could arrest her, and this case could be solved. In time, I hoped, that would bring closure for Cleo and her family.

Most of the tourists in town must have been having their own lunches because there was only one customer in the gift shop when I went in. I wandered past a display of strongly scented candles, including one that made me sneeze, and over to some glass paperweights. I gazed at the swirling colors, wondering if my mom would like one for her birthday, and waited for the shopper to leave.

The customer talked on and on, telling the woman at the counter all about how she and her husband had visited the local winery and describing every variety they sampled. I left the paperweights and rounded the end of the aisle, glancing over at the woman at the counter, who I assumed was Sandy.

"Are you doing all right there?" she called out to me.

I nodded.

She ran a hand over her dark, messy bun and gave me a please-be-patient smile. She was maybe ten years older than me and had a runner's body and lines around her eyes, as if she'd spent a lot of time out in the sun.

I took a few steps past the paperweights and inhaled sharply. There, on the top shelf, was a little ceramic village, like a Christmas village, only the buildings were miniature replicas of the buildings on Main Street in Dogwood Springs. Instead of evergreens and fake snow, the scene was decorated with tiny maple trees and silk dogwood blossoms. The lower display shelves held rows of each type of building: the town hall, the big Methodist church with the white steeple, the three-story library, the bakery, the café, the candy shop, the gift shop, and my favorite, the accessory shop called It Always Fits with its fuchsia-and-white striped awning. Tucked behind an extra library, I even found a miniature copy of the Dogwood Springs History Museum.

I plucked up the museum, checked the price, and quickly decided that it was going home with me. But—

"Can I help you with anything?" The woman from the counter appeared at my side. I'd been so charmed by the little buildings that I hadn't even heard her walk up.

"I love these." I introduced myself as the new museum director and learned she was indeed Sandy Byers. "I'm getting the museum for myself, but I want to get one for my mom, too. She grew up here. Which would you think she'd like for her birthday, the town hall or the library?"

Sandy tapped a finger on the library. "I'd get this one. It sells out the fastest, and we don't always have it in. That way, if you want to get her another part of the village for Christmas or Mother's Day, you'll already have the one that's hardest to get."

"Perfect." I carefully picked up a library.

"And here." She lifted a box off the bottom shelf. "This is a set of maple trees and dogwood blossoms. You could open it and split it between your display and what you give your mom until you both have more buildings. Then you can always buy another box. Would you like me to carry it up to the register for you?"

"Oh, thank you. My mom will love the library." I looked down at the tiny museum. "And I bet I'll have the whole downtown in my living room before the year is out." I could already picture them on my fireplace mantel. Somehow, though, I needed to switch the conversation to the murder. "I, uh, I just love living here. Even though I was pretty upset Saturday when I went to Marjorie Billington's auction. I'd met Sheila Dillon the night before and…" I looked away, hoping my topic shift was subtle enough.

"You poor thing." Sandy patted my arm. "You haven't had a very easy first few months in town. I heard about what happened at the auction, and I read about what happened at the museum earlier in the summer in the paper." She led the way up to the counter.

"Were you at the auction Saturday?"

"No," she answered quickly.

Was I imagining it, or had her muscles tensed? And Danny said he'd seen her there.

"My, uh, my assistant and I came in extra early to unpack a shipment of those paperweights you were looking at. And then, well, Saturday is our biggest day at the shop."

That did make sense. Maybe Danny had seen someone else and thought it was her?

She told me the total, and I slid my credit card into the machine.

"I hope the police find the killer soon. A murder in town can't be good for tourism." She bit her lower lip as she handed me my purchase.

I agreed and left. So much for my optimism. Maybe she was lying, but my gut told me that Sandy didn't care much about Sheila or her family, just herself and her business. And that didn't make her a killer.

Plus, she was right. Another murder in town was bound to affect tourism.

And visits to the museum.

One more reason for me to find Sheila's murderer.

I needed to get back to work, but as soon as I was able, I wanted to learn more about Lisa Brown.

It was cloudy that afternoon, and it never did get very hot, a rare cooler August day in Dogwood Springs. After work, I walked home, gave Bella a big hug, and scratched behind her ears.

She gave one short bark and then stood in front of the fireplace and whined.

"I've already called the landlord, Bella. That's all I can do. He called back while I was at work and said he'd send someone to see if there was an animal in the chimney, but that it may take a while. You'll just have to try to ignore it." I changed into shorts and tennis shoes and picked up her leash. "It really is nice out."

She was at the door before I was.

I opened it, and she wriggled past me.

We took the long route for our walk, and Bella seemed extra energetic. Given all her fur, she was probably enjoying the cooler weather. I did my best to keep up with her and contemplated what approach to take with Lisa Brown.

I had her address. I could—with Cleo or Alice or Zeke— drive to the little town where she lived and show up on her doorstep.

That would be weird.

I could call, but most likely, since she wouldn't recognize my number, she wouldn't pick up.

So, what to say in a message?

Well, I could tell her I was from the museum and

wanted to talk with her about the armoire that we had both been looking at when we were at the auction.

That also seemed a shade creepy since we hadn't even introduced ourselves. It might discourage her from calling me back.

Finally, I decided to simply phone her, leave my name and number, tell her I was calling about the auction, and ask her to return my call.

Once she did, I could explain that I was calling on behalf of the museum, discuss the armoire, and hopefully get a feel for whether she might have killed Sheila.

I stopped, pulled my phone from my back pocket, and dialed. As I expected, she didn't pick up. Hopefully, she would call back soon.

Until she did, though, I was stuck.

I thought for a few minutes, then texted Cleo, Alice, and Zeke and suggested we get together Sunday to try to figure out what to do next.

On Sunday evening, the four of us gathered at our favorite table in the corner of the outdoor seating area at the Dogwood Café. Bella stretched out in the corner near the fence and drank water from a portable bowl I'd brought along.

I ordered a Reuben and coleslaw, Alice had a salad with fat free dressing, and Zeke and Cleo had fries and matching bacon cheeseburgers, except that Zeke's was a double burger.

Alice poured dressing over her salad. "I've got one bit of news, the coroner's findings."

"Excellent." I leaned in. Like Cleo, Alice knew almost everyone in town. And everyone liked her and trusted her. It was no wonder she was a great source of information.

Alice jiggled the little plastic dressing cup, got out a final drop, and set the cup down. She looked glumly at her salad, then at Cleo's burger, and then back up at us. "As you suspected from what she was wearing, Sheila was killed early Saturday morning." She laid a hand on Cleo's arm and spoke more softly. "The coroner says she was hit over the head with a blunt object and then smothered."

Cleo blinked and turned away.

The back of my throat ached. I still felt bad that Cleo was involved in the investigation. It might be what she wanted, but clearly, it was painful for her. "Cleo, I'm so sorry. Sheila didn't deserve that."

"No, she didn't," Cleo said firmly. "And no matter who did this to her, we're going to figure it out."

"I certainly hope so." I petted Bella, who was sniffing near Cleo's plate. "Lie down, girl. The vet says you're not supposed to eat people food."

She settled to the concrete floor with a loud snuffle.

I looked back up. "The timing of the murder might affect our suspect list. Although by the time I got there, the house wasn't locked. Anyone could wander in to view the items up for sale."

"True." Alice speared a cherry tomato. "But it makes more sense that she was killed early, maybe even before Jeannie and Carl opened the house to the public."

"If only we could figure out who the killer was. Because none of our suspects seems to have a good motive." I ran through them one by one. Rick was in love with Sheila. Jeannie seemed to really miss her. Sandy didn't seem to care about Sheila one way or another, only about her business. And Danny would have wanted her alive so that the auction could have gone on. "And I tried calling Lisa Brown, but she hasn't called me back."

"So, no real progress?" Cleo said glumly.

"None." I took a bite of my Reuben and explained that I thought a pushier approach with Lisa might backfire.

"Well, we can't give up," Alice said. "We just have to keep thinking about this, and I'm sure we'll figure it out."

I set my sandwich back down and wiped a glob of thousand island dressing off my hand. "I did have one idea. We ruled out Josh automatically. Maybe that was a mistake. I mean, he was right there almost as soon as I found Sheila's body."

"Uhhnt-uh," Zeke mumbled, then chewed vigorously.

Except for two French fries, his plate was empty.

"No way," Zeke said. "I've known Josh for years. Besides, you never even talked to Mr. Wilson, just assumed he was innocent because of what his wife said."

"That is true," Alice admitted.

Zeke grabbed his last two fries. "You know, Josh's

brother said something one time that made me think Josh didn't like Mr. Wilson very much. Maybe there's a reason."

"We need to talk to him." Cleo sat up taller. "I'll call him tomorrow."

Zeke inhaled the fries and shook his head. "Let me talk to him, see what I can find out."

Most likely, Zeke was right. We didn't want Josh to feel like we were ganging up on him. "That would be great, Zeke. Thank you."

"So, we do nothing? We just wait?" Cleo crossed her arms over her chest.

"I guess so," I said. "And we hope that Lisa calls me back or that Zeke can learn something from Josh."

Clearly, it wasn't the answer Cleo wanted.

But at the moment, it was all we could do.

Chapter Ten

TUESDAY AFTERNOON, just as Imani and I were finishing plans for the museum's fall programming, my cell phone rang from inside my purse in my desk drawer.

I pulled it out. "Odd. Cleo's never called me at work before." Occasionally a text, of course, but...

"I'll get out of here, so you can take that." Imani gathered her papers and left as I answered the call.

"Libby?" Cleo sounded like she was crying.

"What's wrong?"

"Mom asked me to come out to Sheila's house to get her Bible. Sheila highlighted her favorite passages, and Mom thought we could use one in the memorial service."

"That seems like a good plan."

"It was. Except when I got here, I found that someone had broken in and stolen stuff and trashed the place. I'm waiting outside with an officer, and Detective Harper is on his way."

"Oh, no. Do you want me to come over?"

"No. I don't think they'd want that. I imagine the fewer people walking around leaving footprints, the better. I just wanted to know if you'd be home when I got there. I don't want to go into another empty house."

"Absolutely." I reached for the power button on my computer and switched it off. "I'll leave right now and"—I thought for a second—"how about I make us both some tomato soup and grilled cheese sandwiches for dinner?" I wasn't a huge fan of soup in the summer, but it was the most comforting meal I could think of.

"That sounds good, I guess. I'm not really hungry." Her voice was thin and shaky.

"Understandable, but you may be once the shock wears off."

"Yeah, you're probably right."

"I'll leave right away." I wanted to be sure to be there before she got home. And Bella would be there too. Even if I couldn't find the right words to calm Cleo, Bella's presence would help.

It wasn't quite five, but I scooped up my purse, told Imani what had happened, and asked her to lock up when she left.

Not long after that, Cleo and I sat down at my dining table.

Bella brought her favorite toy, a half-chewed-up stuffed

chicken, and dropped it at Cleo's feet, one of her strongest expressions of support.

Cleo gave the drooly chicken a skeptical glance and, instead of picking it up, patted Bella's head.

After a moment, Cleo turned to face the table, and Bella flopped onto the floor between us.

I passed Cleo a plate of grilled cheese sandwiches, cut into triangle-shaped quarters.

"You were right." Cleo, who had been texting with her mom, set her phone down. "That does smell good."

"I'm glad." I opened a sleeve of saltines. "Did your mom have any news?"

"Not really. Detective Harper came by to talk to her, to see when she'd last been out at Sheila's, but that was more than a week ago."

Cleo passed back the sandwiches.

I took two triangles, then crushed up three saltines and added them to my soup. "So, all the police know is that the break-in happened sometime between when Sheila left for the auction early Saturday morning and this afternoon, when you went to her house? What about neighbors? Would they have seen anything?"

"I doubt it." Cleo took some crackers. "Sheila's house is out in the country. You really can't see the neighbors."

"Oh. Well, were you able to tell what was taken?" I took a bite of grilled cheese.

"Some of it was obvious. Her TV was gone, and her laptop, and a fancy coffee maker. And I'm pretty sure she had some nice diamond earrings that weren't in her jewelry box. I doubt she wore them to the auction. For everyday, she liked big, dangly earrings."

"I could see that. Small earrings wouldn't really go with her style. So did Detective Harper think the break-in was connected to the murder?"

"No. He thinks it was done by the same thieves who are targeting stores downtown."

"Maybe." I stopped, a spoonful of soup halfway to my mouth. "But have you heard of any other burglaries in homes?"

"Not a one. Actually, I haven't heard of any burglaries at all since the day before Sheila was killed."

"Me either. And no offense to Sheila, but I'm guessing her house wasn't the fanciest in town or the one with the nicest electronics."

"Not at all. Just a plain, ordinary, three-bedroom ranch. She'd worked hard all her life and was proud that her house was paid off, but she wasn't rich."

I frowned. "I guess there might be things we don't know about, similarities between the break-in at Sheila's house and the ones downtown, but the timing seems suspicious to me."

Cleo took a sip of her Diet Dr. Pepper and nodded. "It does to me too. And it makes me mad that not only did this person kill my favorite cousin, but they also trashed her house. Mom and I will have to clean all that up, and it's just going to upset her."

"I can help clean, and I bet Alice would help too. Your mom wouldn't have to do anything."

"Oh, Libby, that is so nice of you. I'll talk to my mom, but I might take you up on your offer." Cleo's eyes welled with tears, and she blinked them away. "Of course, we have to wait until the police are done collecting evidence."

"I understand." I remembered all too well how long that had taken after the murder at the museum. "In the meantime, we can focus on finding the killer. This person needs to be caught."

"You've got that right," Cleo said. "Sheila didn't deserve this. And neither did our family."

No, they didn't. If there was any way I could figure out the culprit, that person would be brought to justice.

Chapter Eleven

THE NEXT EVENING, around seven, I was doing a crossword when my phone dinged with a text.

I glanced over at it.

It was Sam.

My heart rate shot up, and I grabbed the phone.

Hi, Libby. Sorry it took so long to get back to you. My dad had a health issue, and I've been in St. Louis a lot the past few weeks. I got the painting back from the restorer. Still interested in seeing it and going to dinner?

Aww. His dad had been sick.

But I was pretty sure his cell phone would have worked in St. Louis. I also had to imagine he'd had at least two free moments in the past few weeks to send a text to say hi. And nowhere in that message did he use the word "date."

Maybe I'd misunderstood earlier this summer. Maybe his intention all along had been a business dinner.

Which was exactly how I was going to treat it.

"That's logical. Right, Bella?"

Bella, who would score at the top of the extroversion scale on any personality test, might not have been the best one to ask. She looked up at me with a doggie smile that seemed to say that Sam was probably a great guy. That my ex-husband was an anomaly and that I should be more trusting. That if I was going to make a real life for myself here in Dogwood Springs, I needed to move past my divorce and give Sam a chance.

I ignored her.

Business. Dinner.

My fingers flew over the screen.

Sure. Hope your dad is doing better.

A few seconds later, Sam texted again.

Dad's fine now. Thanks for asking. Is there any chance you'd be free for dinner Saturday? I could pick you up at 7 if that works for you.

My turn.

7 sounds good.

I hit send, trying hard to focus on the fact that the museum might be getting a real Clayton Smithton painting. And not on the fact that there was no reason for Sam to pick me up for a business dinner.

"So, how much do you trust me?" Cleo raised the hair salon chair and caught my gaze in the mirror.

I'd been swamped at work and barely seen her since

Sam asked me out. Today, despite the fact that it was Saturday, her busiest day of the week, she'd insisted on working me in, saying she couldn't look at my split ends anymore.

My stomach tightened ever so slightly. "What are you thinking?"

"Well, you're going out with the most eligible bachelor in town tonight. So we really want you looking your best. And he lived in California, so everything here probably seems rather dull. How about something like this?" She held up a lock of my hair and slid two fingers around it like a pair of scissors an inch away from my scalp.

I backed away. "It's a business dinner."

Cleo rolled her eyes. "He's picking you up. It's a date."

"And you said a trim, not something totally different."

She burst out laughing. "I'm kidding. Seriously, Libby, you need to relax. I'm good at what I do."

"I know that. It's just that I've had the same haircut and gone to the same woman back in Philly for years. And since I moved here and realized how humid Missouri is in the summer, I haven't even had it trimmed. I've been liking the extra length because I can put it in a ponytail."

"I've noticed." She narrowed her eyes, and her forehead furrowed. "You don't need all this length for a ponytail. And we're doing some caramel highlights, right?"

"I guess." Cleo had shown me photos of the color she wanted to add, but I couldn't really envision it on me. Plus, the one time I'd colored my hair, when I decided to go red in college and did it myself, had been a big mistake. Maybe it was the wrong shade of red? I wasn't sure, but it had made my face look sort of green. I'd gone to a salon and paid to have it dyed back to brown a week later.

I repositioned myself in the salon chair, unable to get comfortable.

"Aww, Libby, you're really stressing over this. I didn't mean to freak you out. We don't have to change anything. I can simply take an inch off the ends and leave your cut exactly as it has been, if you want. But I can honestly tell you that of all the people who let me do what I thought would flatter them most, I've never had a single unhappy client in Dogwood Springs. And I promise I would leave you enough hair for a ponytail, but it would be a short one."

I stared at myself in the mirror. Pale skin, big green eyes, and dark brown hair two inches past my shoulders. I looked … fine. Not my best. Not even as good as I had back in Philly after I'd seen my regular stylist. I did want to look nice representing the museum when I had dinner with Sam. More importantly, I wanted to make this new chapter of my life here in Dogwood Springs the best chapter of my life so far. I didn't want my best days to be before the divorce, before I lost my job back in Philadelphia, before I turned thirty.

I sat up taller and turned to face Cleo. "Do it. Leave me enough for a ponytail, but other than that, do whatever you think best."

A grin burst across her face. "Excellent! I've been wanting to work on your hair since the first day I met you." She picked up a comb and began sectioning.

After sitting with enough foil in my hair to scare children at Halloween, a shampoo, and time spent with some vanilla-scented deep conditioner, she led me back to the salon chair and cut off a huge chunk of my hair.

Under the plastic cape, I winced. "Ponytail?" I pleaded.

"I didn't promise a long ponytail," she said in a soothing tone. "Trust me."

I shut my eyes. Even with Cleo, who had become a dear friend, trust wasn't the easiest thing for me. That last year in Philly, with the divorce, had just been too ugly. Oh, I didn't think Cleo would lie to me. I simply wasn't sure that her idea of what would look good was the same as mine. "I won't have to spend lots of time curling it every day, will I?"

"Nope. A quick blow-dry, and you should be good. But some beachy waves would be cute for your date."

"It's not a date."

"Uh-huh. You keep saying that. But if a guy asks you out to dinner, it's a date. Business is done over lunch."

Another chopped-off hunk of hair hit my shoulder on its way to the floor. I opened one eye.

One side of my hair was significantly shorter than the other side but still almost to my shoulder. I closed both eyes again.

Eventually, Cleo stopped cutting. "You should probably open your eyes now, Libby. Watch how I start drying at the roots, not the ends, to build volume. And this stuff is great for protecting your hair." She grabbed a squirt from a bottle on the counter and held her hand near my nose. "See how good it smells?"

It was nice. Like coconut.

She worked it through my hair and began using the blow dryer.

"Did you want me to help clean up things at Sheila's house?" I asked, eyes still shut.

"No. Mom decided to hire a professional cleaner. She and I'll go in a week or so and clear out Sheila's stuff. But thanks for offering."

A professional cleaner was probably a good idea. I knew from the murder at the museum that fingerprint powder wasn't always easy to clean.

Finally, Cleo turned off the dryer, ran her fingers through my hair, and trimmed a tiny bit on one side. Then she set a mirror in my lap and slowly spun me around.

I opened my eyes, and a tingle ran through me. My hair, once a plain dark brown, now had more variation in color, more depth, and was slightly lighter overall. The lighter shade flattered my complexion, making me look less pale, and instead of simply hanging on either side of my face, the hair framed my features and moved gracefully when I tilted my head.

Unable to stop, I tipped my head to one side, then the other. I didn't say it out loud, but I thought I looked like a model. Okay, not a model's face, but a model's hair. I handed the mirror back to Cleo. "It looks amazing. I can't believe it's me."

"It's you." She gave one side a little fluff.

"Can you take the cape off?"

She did.

And I leapt out of the chair and hugged her.

Chapter Twelve

AT SIX THAT EVENING, I gave Bella her dinner and slid on
the outfit I'd picked out before my haircut—narrow white
pants, a navy and white striped top, and dressy navy
sandals. I put the Eagles' *Hotel California* album on the
stereo that had been my dad's in college, did my makeup,
and admired my hair, watching how it moved in the mirror
when I tipped my head. I let Bella out for a few minutes,
told her I'd be home early, and gave her a dog biscuit.

Five minutes before Sam was due to pick me up, I
turned off the music and sat down on the couch.

And then, as if I'd only been calm because of Don
Henley's voice, the jitters hit, and my stomach tightened.

Oh, I'd enjoyed talking with Sam when we met a few
weeks ago. But most of that evening, I'd thought of Sam as
the person who bought my grandparents' home and
someone who wanted to donate a painting to the museum,

not a potential date. I'd felt comfortable and easily made conversation.

But tonight, despite the fact that I'd denied it to Cleo, was a date. A date with the most eligible bachelor in Dogwood Springs, possibly the most eligible bachelor in the whole state. After all, how many men made a fortune in tech in California and relocated to a small town in Missouri? Or anywhere in Missouri?

And why would he want to date me? My ex had dumped me for a younger woman who, if I was pressed, I had to admit was also prettier and smarter than me.

I let out a dejected sigh. "Oh, Bella, this is a mistake." I was going to get hurt. Again.

She trotted over and licked my hand.

Bella, at least, loved me. Sure, she loved everyone, but I knew, beyond a shadow of a doubt, that she would never abandon me for an owner who was younger, prettier, or smarter. Even though I'd only adopted her two months ago, I was her human, the one who mattered more to her than anyone else.

Just like I'd once thought I mattered to my ex.

Aargh! What was I doing, setting myself up for disappointment and heartache? And if Sam interacted with the museum, which, given his millions, I had to hope he would, I could also look forward to awkward situations. I should have suggested we meet at a restaurant. For lunch. This was a mistake, a horrible, horrible mis—

The doorbell rang.

Bella gave an encouraging woof and galloped over to the

door, more than ready to meet whoever might be on the other side.

I followed, much more slowly, and opened the door to the entryway and then the front door of the house.

"Hi." Sam stood on the front step.

My mouth went dry. "Hi." He seemed taller than I remembered, at least six feet, and I smelled the faintest hint of his cologne or soap, something outdoorsy. His dark hair was perfectly cut, his brown eyes twinkled behind his rectangular glasses, and his tan pants and navy polo-style shirt had that effortless perfection that comes from expensive fabric and expert tailoring. There was no way he bought his polos from the same mail-order catalog as my ex.

"It's great to see you, Libby. You look wonderful."

Warmth filled my chest. "Thank you. It's great to see you too. You—"

Bella wiggled past me, sniffed Sam, and rubbed her head against his leg.

"Bella, stop. You'll get dog hair all over Sam's pants."

But Sam had already knelt down with his face close to hers, saying hello.

Bella licked his cheek.

"Bella!"

Sam ran a hand along her back. "Aw, aren't you the best dog ever?" He stood back up, grinning. "You didn't tell me you had a golden retriever! We had one when I was growing up. He was my best friend." He gave an awkward shrug. "I wasn't exactly the most popular kid. More like the school's biggest geek."

"Bella is a sweetheart." I gestured toward the door to my apartment. "I've only had her for a couple of months, since I moved here. Come on in and let me get her settled before we leave."

Bella galloped over to the fireplace and looked back at Sam.

He gave her a quizzical look but followed her.

As soon as he got close to the hearth, she began barking. Loudly.

"Bella!" I said firmly. "Stop!"

She ignored me and kept barking.

"Sam, I'm so sorry. I think there's a squirrel up there. It's almost like every person who comes into the apartment, she has to warn them."

Sam leaned down and looked Bella in the eye. "Big bad squirrel?"

She barked louder.

I made an awkward gesture with my hands. "I, uh, I guess we'd better go."

Sam walked toward the door. "Probably for the best. I have a surprise planned for dinner." He pressed two fingers against his lips, as if afraid his secret might slip out.

In that instant, the tightness in my stomach eased. Because how nervous could I be around a guy who'd planned a surprise? A guy who just told me he was unpopular as a kid? A guy whose perfectly cut hair was now styled with a little dog drool?

～

"So, what's the surprise? Where are we having dinner?" I settled into Sam's blue Tesla, trying not to stare at the dashboard with its giant screen.

"You'll have to wait and see." Sam turned to me, his eyes twinkling, then looked back at Elm Street. "But I hope you don't mind that I need to make a quick stop on campus before we eat."

"A quick stop won't be a problem. Tell me about the painting." The work was a real mystery, with part of the picture added later by another artist.

"As I told you before, the restorer is convinced the original painting really is a Clayton Smithton, and he was able to remove the newer paint. It looks like a family portrait except that someone had later altered it to paint out the older daughter."

"Fascinating." The historian in me was dying to know more. "I can't wait to see it now that it's restored."

"I've got it for a few days, and then I've made arrangements to ship it to Halbrook and Klein next week for independent confirmation and to get a valuation done for tax purposes."

"Excellent." Halbrook and Klein had a great reputation. If they were involved, and if Sam went ahead with his plans to donate it to the museum, I could give him whatever paperwork he needed for tax purposes with no problem.

Sam took Elm south toward Grove University. "Then I hope to officially donate the painting to the Dogwood Springs History Museum, if you'll accept it."

"With pleasure." Excitement filled my chest. "A work by

a well-known American artist will make a fabulous addition to the museum."

"Great. That's where it should be. How have things been going there, after the murder?"

"A bit rocky at first, but things are looking up." I omitted the bleak attendance records and instead told him about the visit from the children at the community center and our plans for the town birthday party.

He stopped at a light. "If I can get the painting back in time, would it help the event if you could add it to the museum that day?"

I drew in a sharp breath. "Oh, that would be wonderful. I know it would increase turnout at the event and probably draw a lot of press."

"Then I'll have to try to make that happen."

I looked over at him. "Thank you."

He smiled at me, then went through the light, drove through the maze of the university that I could only navigate with GPS, and pulled into a parking lot by a building with a cupola on top, which I recognized as the main administration building of the campus. "Why don't you come in with me?" he said. "This may take a few minutes, and the car will be sweltering."

Hmmm. I would think I could just sit here with the AC on, but maybe he didn't trust me with his Tesla. "Okay."

Inside, Sam led me down the hall. "I just need to check something that was left for me near the president's office."

Hopefully, this wouldn't take long. I was so hungry that

I could swear I smelled Italian food. Wishful smelling, I guess.

Sam stopped in an area open to the floors above, which I thought was under the cupola.

"It's supposed to be in here." Sam pulled a single key from his pants pocket. He unlocked a door to our left, and I followed him into a plush conference room.

Inside, one end of the table was spread with a red-checkered tablecloth. A covered breadbasket, along with two place settings, several covered dishes, and a carafe of iced tea sat waiting. The scent of garlic and tomatoes and cheese was so strong that my mouth watered.

I turned to Sam. "Are we—are we eating here?"

"We are. I thought you might like to be the first to see the new book that's on display." He gestured to a glass case at the end of the room.

There, along with a portrait that was a twin of one we had at the museum, was a book about my great-great-grand-mother, Elsie Dorsett.

I rushed toward the case to get a better look. "Oh! I knew it was being written, but I had no idea it was out."

"The author is on sabbatical, so she asked me to give you this." Sam handed me a copy of the book, *One Woman's Legacy*.

I took the book and found the author's signature inside. Then I looked from the book to the display to dinner. "I can't believe you arranged all this."

"Once I got my head slightly above water with my dad's business, I felt terrible about how much time had passed since I said I'd call. He owns a landscaping firm, and those first couple of weeks working on job sites nearly killed me. I fell into bed every night as soon as I showered and ate dinner."

"Oh, my."

"He thought it was hilarious. Said I'd gone soft. Anyway, I hoped being the first to see this display might help you forgive me." He gestured to the table. "Please, sit. We should eat before the food gets cold."

"Of course I forgive you." I sat in the chair he held out for me. "And this is such a treat."

"Your great-great grandmother must have been quite a woman." Sam turned and opened a cooler that sat on a low table along the wall. "Salad?"

"Please." I unrolled the silverware from the napkin that lay diagonally in front of me, making a space for Sam to set down a chilled salad plate. "She was, but how did you do all this?"

"They don't advertise it, but La Villetta caters."

"Oh." I bet any place catered if someone as rich as Sam Collins made the request.

"And there's a guy on the weekend cleaning crew who let them in while I picked you up. His wife runs a business from their home, and I helped her with a computer virus once, so Raoul is always asking if there is anything he can do to help me." Sam held the breadbasket toward me. "Since he was going to be in the building anyway, I figured it wouldn't be too much of an inconvenience for him to let them in."

I took a bite of my salad. I'd been to La Villetta once, for a celebration of my aunt and uncle's wedding anniversary. The creamy Italian dressing tasted exactly the same—incredible. "Yum."

That was me, fabulous conversationalist. Surely, I could step up my game.

I speared a piece of tomato and some lettuce from my salad. "Tell me about yourself. What made you decide to move to Dogwood Springs?"

"I used to work in the tech sector. At first, it was incredibly fun. After a while, though, I got bored." He lifted the lids of three small chafing dishes, revealing lasagna, seafood Alfredo, and eggplant parmesan.

"So you decided to teach?" I helped myself to some lasagna and a small serving of eggplant parmesan and leaned in, eager to hear more.

"Yeah. I didn't really want to go back to school to get a teaching degree, or my Ph.D., but Grove University was happy to have me as an adjunct, teaching computer science. Plus, I'm closer to my family in St. Louis."

I thought of his family and realized that Sam could easily have bankrolled any lost income when his dad was ill. The fact that he'd instead gone out on the job sites as a laborer said a lot about him. "Do you like teaching?"

"I love it. And I love being here in Dogwood Springs. I think I was ready for a slower pace."

"It is nice," I said. "I wasn't thrilled to be here at first. I kind of thought I should be at a big museum in some urban area, but this town grows on you fast. The people here are so nice."

Sam looked up at me and our eyes met. "They are. There are people here you can really be comfortable with." The corners of his lips turned up, and a warm smile spread across his face.

My pulse sped. Suddenly, my heart felt as gooey as the cheese in the lasagna. Good heavens. That smile of his was dangerous.

I exhaled and glanced down at my plate, trying to get my pulse to return to a normal pace.

"So, tell me about your life." He leaned back in his chair. "I imagine things got a lot calmer after the murderer was caught."

"Well, actually..." And so I told him about Sheila's death, about how I'd found the body, and about how my friends and I were trying to figure out who the killer was.

Sam's eyes widened. "I'm so sorry you had to find another body, Libby. I didn't even know. I've been out of town so much." He shook his head. "You seem to have mysteries everywhere you go. The museum, the auction, even the painting."

"Ooh, the painting." I gestured to the dinner. "This meal is fabulous, but I do want to see the restored painting."

"I have it over in my office. We can walk over after dinner and take a look." Sam sipped his iced tea and topped off both our glasses from the carafe on the table. "I do wonder about the girl who was painted out of the portrait. Do you think we could figure out who she was?"

"Well, up in the storage room, the museum has copies of the photos that were taken on the first day of school each year at the Silersville School."

"Silersville?"

"That was the name of this town until my great-great-grandmother pushed through a motion to change it. She said a beautiful town needed a beautiful name and that with the spring so close, the name should be the same."

"She rebranded it." Sam chuckled.

"She did. Although I don't know if they had that word back then." From what I'd read, the name change made a few people mad, but it had been key to transforming the town. "Anyway, if we find the school photo from the right year, we should be able to learn that girl's name."

"Now that sounds like a lot of fun," Sam said. "I'll be in St. Louis for the next couple of days. Promise you won't look without me?"

I hesitated, suddenly keen to look up those archived photos. But to be fair, it was Sam's painting. "I promise."

After that, the evening flew by. The meal was fantastic. I took photos of the new display about Elsie to send to my mom and my aunts. And we walked over and saw the restored painting. Where once there had been what appeared to be an image of a mother, father, and daughter, with the city hall seen out a window, now appeared to be a family of four, with no window. The girl who had been painted out looked to be about fifteen or sixteen, and she resembled her father far more than her mother or younger sister.

Sam and I talked about our favorite restaurants in town, great vacations we'd taken, and what our dreams were for the future. I even admitted my love of tea and shortbread and learned that Sam was secretly addicted to that pricy, gourmet ice cream brand, Minnesota's Pride, particularly the chocolate cheesecake flavor.

All in all, a lovely evening.

At last, when the sky was a deep blue, almost black, Sam drove me home and walked me to my door.

As we drew near, a muffled woof came from inside. Bella's face appeared in the living room window, peering out at the two of us under the porch light.

Sam chuckled and stepped closer, looking down at me. "I hope Bella doesn't mind if I kiss you goodnight."

A fluttery feeling filled my veins. "I, uh, I think she'd be okay with it."

He slid an arm around my waist. "I had a great time tonight, Libby."

"Me too." And I had, in spite of my earlier fears. I gazed up into his brown eyes.

He threaded his hand into the hair at the base of my neck.

Suddenly, the air around us felt charged with electricity. The hum of cicadas, the wheeze of my window unit air-conditioner, and the occasional rumble of a car rolling down Elm Street faded away. Nothing mattered but Sam and me.

My heart pounded. Slowly, as if pulled by an invisible force, I leaned in.

And he brought his lips to mine.

If I said that planets may have realigned at that moment, it would probably sound ridiculous. Suffice it to say that a few moments later, when I stepped back and looked at Sam, my knees were wobbly.

He appeared just as stunned.

We mumbled a rather dazed goodnight, and I went inside and sank back against the door.

The planets may not have realigned, but my world had certainly just spun off its axis—in the best possible way.

Chapter Thirteen

EARLY THE NEXT MORNING, before the day got hot, I took Bella on a walk downtown. She was in her element, greeting every person we met, and I, well, I may have been mooning over Sam just a bit. But at least I was getting some exercise while I did it.

Since it was Sunday, most of the shops were closed until noon, but the restaurants were open for brunch, and the outside seating at the café was packed, with two groups of people standing near the hostess stand, discussing how good the pancakes smelled.

I inhaled deeply as Bella and I walked by. "Personally, it's the bacon that smells good to me, girl. What do you think?"

Bella gave a soft woof, which I took as agreement.

A block farther down the street, near a restaurant with a popular brunch buffet, I drew in a quick breath.

Coming out of the restaurant was the woman from the

auction, Lisa Brown. Her leopard-print purse was slung over her shoulder.

She and another woman stopped on the sidewalk and hugged. They went through a long, dramatic goodbye filled with many promises to get together again soon. From what they said, I gathered they each lived about two hours away, but in opposite directions.

I pretended to look at items in the window of the accessory store, all the while keeping an eye on Lisa. The minute she was done with her reunion, I had some questions to ask her.

Finally, after one last hug, the other woman turned away and headed up the street.

Lisa turned toward me.

Now was my chance. Subtle. Remember to be subtle.

"Oh, hello." I put myself directly in her path. Bella cooperated fully, turning her body perpendicular to the flow of the sidewalk.

Lisa's over-plucked eyebrows pinched together, and a fuzzy look came into her eyes.

"We met at the auction." I stepped closer. "Well, we didn't actually meet, but I saw you in the room with the armoire."

"Oh, yes!" Lisa's face lit, then dimmed. "Such a tragic event."

"It certainly was. I'm Libby Ballard, by the way." I stuck out a hand. "I'm the director of the local history museum."

"Lisa Brown." She shook my hand. "I'm sorry I never

called you back. I listened to your message and then got distracted and forgot all about it."

"Been there. Done that." Luckily, fate had given me a chance to talk to her in person. "Were you able to buy what you were interested in before the auction was shut down?"

"No. I was actually hoping to buy that armoire." She gave an exaggerated shiver. "I'm not so interested now."

Excellent. Despite the fact that Sheila's body had been hidden in the armoire, the museum still might want it. Maybe. But if we did, I didn't want to be bidding against anyone. "I was interested in that myself. It's not a great piece, but it's got ties to the town founder, and I was hoping to buy it for the museum."

"Really?" Lisa stepped into the shade of a nearby awning. "It's also got ties to me, so I'd be very interested to learn what you know about the history of the piece."

"Ties to you?"

She nodded so hard that her thin, dangling earrings swayed back and forth. "My father, Tobias Brown, lived near here before I was born and had done repair work on the piece."

"On the drawer."

"Exactly. Anyway, my mom died when I was a baby, and my dad raised me on his own. He passed away about a year ago, so anything connected to him is rather special to me. Unless, of course, it's connected to a murder."

That made sense. Except that she wasn't from around here. How had she known to come to Dogwood Springs? "Did the auction house contact you about the piece?"

"No. In early June, I received a letter from the woman whose estate was being auctioned off, Marjorie Billington, asking me to come visit her. She said she wanted to give me an antique armoire that my father had done restoration work on."

"But she didn't?"

"When I called the number she gave, hoping to set up a time to visit, a relative named Danny was at the house. He said Marjorie had died a couple of days before, on the first of June , and that the armoire and all the other antiques would be auctioned off."

I ran a hand over my mouth. "You'd think he would have honored her intentions."

"Yeah, but I guess he really didn't know me. Didn't know if I was telling the truth." She spread her arms in a who-knows expression. "Anyway, I kept an eye on local auctions online. When the Billington auction was announced, I decided to come and see the armoire. I went to the preview on Friday night, and I found a note on the back that my dad had typed, which was so like him, always meticulous. After I saw that, I decided to stay in town overnight and try to buy the armoire."

Everything she said sounded believable. But she'd looked so ill at ease when I walked into the room with the armoire that morning. Most likely, it wasn't a good idea to mention that she'd looked guilty. "I, um, I actually wondered if you were okay that morning. You seemed upset."

"Upset?" Her forehead wrinkled, then she rolled her

eyes. "Oh, I was upset all right." She let out a snort. "I'd just gotten a text from my husband. He'd heard from the contractor. Can you believe they want almost $10,000 to redo our roof?" Her jaw tightened. "I'm tempted to climb up there and reroof it myself, except it's so darned steep." She blew out a breath. "Well, that and the fact that I know nothing about roofing."

"That does seem like a lot of money."

"Highway robbery, if you ask me. Anyway, if I looked odd, that's why. It certainly wasn't because I killed that poor woman." She gave a loud laugh, as if she had never even imagined that I'd suspected her.

Probably, it had been foolish.

But at this point, I'd talked to all our suspects, and I was no closer to figuring out who the killer was.

Either the murder had been committed by a person we hadn't thought of...

Or someone was lying.

Chapter Fourteen

THAT AFTERNOON, Sam texted to tell me how much he'd enjoyed our date. I replied that I had as well. After we chatted back and forth a bit, I may have let out a few sighs worthy of a teenage girl as I lay on the couch daydreaming.

Later, while Bella and I were watching *Antiques Road-show*, I got another interesting text, this time from Zeke. He said he'd been talking with Josh, the kid who worked at the auction house, and that if I was willing to meet the two of them in a neighborhood park in the eastern part of town, Josh had information I needed to hear.

I quickly texted back, and we agreed to be at the park at three thirty.

I couldn't wait to hear what Josh might have to say.

Maybe he'd heard more than Jeannie had about the situation with Sandy Byers. Maybe he'd even heard Sandy threaten Sheila about the antique photos. Or maybe he'd seen Rick at the house the morning of the auction. Maybe the story Rick told had been one big lie. Maybe he and Sheila had argued.

Finally, a little after three, I shut off the TV. "Ready for a drive, girl?"

Bella nudged her leash off the hook where I kept it in the kitchen and carried it to me. No offense to the dog we'd had when I was little, but Bella really was the smartest dog ever.

I picked up my purse, and the two of us headed out to my car. "Time to get some answers, girl."

Bella eagerly climbed in, ready to ride shotgun.

Of course, twenty minutes was far more time than I needed to drive to the park. Dogwood Springs wasn't that big.

No one else was there when I arrived. In fact, the park was completely empty. It didn't offer a lot of amenities, just a few swings, a basketball hoop, and a couple of picnic tables, but it did have really nice shade trees. If I'd been a kid in the neighborhood, I'd have been there. But maybe not that many kids lived nearby. Neighborhoods did tend to have waves of children who grew up, only to be replaced by new kids and new families a generation later. Maybe that's why Zeke and Josh had suggested it, knowing it was a private place to talk.

Still, I was fairly new to town. I walked over and looked at the park sign again to be sure I was in the right place.

I was.

Just before three thirty, Zeke arrived on his bike. "No

Josh yet?" He took off his helmet and leaned down to pet Bella.

I shook my head. "But wait, I think I see a car."

"That's him." Zeke leaned his bike against a tree and walked over to meet Josh.

I waved and pointed to a picnic table under a big oak tree.

Zeke gave me a thumbs up, but even after Josh got out of his car, they didn't come right over. The two of them talked for a minute, and I couldn't tell what they were saying, but from the way Zeke gestured toward me, he might still have been convincing Josh that I was safe to talk to.

Eventually, they walked over, Zeke at a normal pace, Josh dragging behind.

"Uh, sorry I was late," he said. "I had to spray the shoes again. My boss said I didn't use enough Lysol. That I actually have to pick them up and stick my thumb inside to lift the tongue, not just spray them while they sit on the counter."

"Spray the shoes?"

"Yeah. I got a new job at the bowling alley." He sat at the picnic table across from me, but at the very edge of the seat.

Bella wriggled up next to him and laid her head on his knee.

He gave her a nervous smile and patted her head.

"I appreciate you coming to talk with us, Josh," I said, using the soft, slow voice that I reserved for shy little kids at the museum. "Sheila seemed like such a good person."

Josh ran a hand over his wispy beard, new since the day of the auction. "Yeah, she was really nice to me. That's why I thought I should come. But now that I'm here..." He glanced toward his car.

Zeke leaned in. "I promise you, man, nobody here is going to tell anyone we heard stuff from you."

I scooted forward on the bench. "Zeke's right, Josh. If you know something, something that might help us find out who killed Sheila, please tell us. We promise we won't mention where we heard it."

I mimed locking my lips.

Josh's shoulders stiffened, then released. "Okay. I need to tell someone, and I have no interest in talking to the cops."

"Josh and his friends got caught spray-painting graffiti on a concrete retaining wall by the high school football field," Zeke said under his breath.

"A harmless prank," Josh said quickly. "There was no need for them to get so bent out of shape. And what we wrote—that the principal could be the school mascot, because he looks so much like a bulldog—was the God's honest truth."

Zeke snickered.

Josh squirmed. "But, anyway, I don't want to talk to the cops after what happened. And I didn't put it together right away, not until I got home because, well, I was kind of freaked out after seeing the body." His ears turned red.

"I was too. I understand," I said.

"But later, I remembered that the day before the auction

preview, Sheila had been really mad. She figured out that Carl was skimming money from each auction, stealing from the customers."

Adrenaline tingled down my arms. "You're kidding."

Josh shook his head. "Not kidding. Not a ton of money, at least not on a small auction. I think it was more like a percentage that he tried to take each time. Sheila told me he'd lost a lot on online sports gambling and owed money to a loan shark. But the Wilsons don't know that I know. And I don't want them to know I told you."

"They won't. I promise," I said. "I can't believe Jeannie acted like she was so sad that Sheila had been killed. She probably knew exactly what her husband had been doing. And when Sheila died, either she and Carl were relieved, thinking their secret was safe, or—"

"Or if they found out that Sheila knew what they were up to, one of them could have been the murderer," Zeke said.

Josh winced.

"I see why you took a job at the Rollerama," Zeke said. "In spite of having to spray the smelly shoes."

We talked for a few more minutes, but Josh didn't know much more.

I reassured Josh once more that I wouldn't mention his name and led Bella toward my car. I texted Alice and Cleo, telling them that, based on what Josh had told Zeke and me, it seemed obvious that Carl was the murderer.

Thanks to Zeke, I'd learned vital information from Josh, information that he'd have never shared with Detective

Harper. The detective could call me nosy all he wanted to, but I was going to be the one who solved this crime.

I'd only driven a few blocks toward home when my phone dinged with a text. Probably Alice or Cleo, asking for more details.

Whoever it was would have to wait. There wasn't much traffic out tonight, but I wasn't going to text and drive.

After several more blocks, my phone dinged again. And then again.

"Good grief, Bella, something must be going on." I pulled over to the side of the road.

My throat tightened as I read a text from Cleo.

I was walking on the bike path near the university, by the glass shop that looks like a silo, and I found Carl Wilson's dead body.

Chapter Fifteen

CLEO HAD TEXTED two more times.

Oh, Libby, this is awful. I think Carl was shot.

And then she added more.

Waiting on police now.

I let out a heavy sigh. Talking to Josh had been a waste of time. We'd totally been on the wrong track. Carl wasn't the killer.

The killer was still out there.

And poor Cleo. Finding a dead body was bad enough. But finding a dead body only days after a family member had been murdered had to be even worse. She didn't need to go through that.

"Change of plans," I said to Bella. "Cleo needs us."

I was still learning Dogwood Springs, so I did a quick internet search on my phone for glass shops in the area. I was expecting a tourist shop that sold stained glass but instead found a store that sold window glass and mirrors and had a logo that looked like a silo. I plugged the address into my GPS and started driving.

After five on a Sunday, the store was closed, the parking lot deserted. I pulled into a spot by the silo and clipped on Bella's leash.

Once we were outside the car, I spotted the bike path, running behind the shop.

But I didn't see Cleo, and I didn't hear anything.

"Cleo?" I yelled.

Nothing.

I started to pull out my phone to text Cleo, but Bella gave a soft bark.

Could Bella tell which way to go? I bet she could. "Bella, find Cleo."

Bella sniffed the air and without hesitation turned left onto the bike path.

We had only walked maybe a hundred feet down the shady path when, off to the right, I saw blue lights flashing.

I broke into a run, and Bella raced ahead, pulling me along.

A police officer appeared from around the curve in the path, one hand held out. "Ma'am, I need you to stop. There's been a crime committed, and we need to preserve the crime scene."

Bella and I lurched to a halt, and I gasped for breath.

I'd met several members of the Dogwood Springs Police Department after the murder at the museum, but this officer was unfamiliar. He was a big, beefy guy with a strawberry blond buzz cut, and young, so young that he might be fresh out of training.

"My friend is there, officer. She texted me after she found the body. I hate for her to be alone."

The officer stood up taller and spread his elbows, blocking the entire path. "No can do, ma'am. Your friend is perfectly safe with the police here. And she's not alone. She's speaking with Detective Harper."

"But..." I stepped to one side and looked around him. Surely, they could make an exception.

"Time to turn around, ma'am. We do not need another set of footprints and a dog at the crime scene."

"But Detective Harper thinks Bella is supersmart. Maybe she could help."

His face grew grim. "And maybe you'd better head home before I take you in to the station."

Fine. Someone was getting a little big for their brand-new police-issue britches. But I turned and gave Bella's leash a gentle tug.

I swatted at a mosquito that flew by my ear, and the two of us walked quickly back to the parking lot. If I couldn't go to Cleo, I wasn't getting eaten.

Once in the car, I texted Alice and Zeke, told them Cleo had found Carl's dead body, and invited them to come to my apartment for an emergency meeting. I included Cleo on the text and told her we'd be waiting there as soon as she was able to come home.

Alice replied immediately, asking if we could meet at her house instead because she had a cake in the oven.

Zeke agreed.

But Cleo didn't reply.

"I guess that makes sense, right, Bella? She's still giving her statement to Detective Harper. She'll see the text and meet us at Alice's."

Alice's husband was allergic to dogs, so I took Bella home, told her she'd done a great job on the bike path and that I would be home soon.

Then I drove to Alice's. I was just going up the steps to her beautiful two-story brick house when my phone dinged with a message from Cleo.

I may be a while. I have to be fingerprinted. Harper thinks I'm a suspect.

Chapter Sixteen

NUMBNESS WASHED over me as Alice opened the door. I held the phone up so she could read the message.

Her lips narrowed to a thin line. "Unbelievable."

"Wh—what?" I sputtered. "What on earth is Detective Harper thinking of, suspecting Cleo of murder?"

From the day I'd moved to Dogwood Springs, Cleo had welcomed me like a long-lost friend. She'd been there for me when I went through the horrible experience of finding a dead body at the museum, and she'd volunteered to help me find the killer and save my job. And she was loved by everyone in town. Good at her job, always upbeat, and from a respected local family.

The idea of her as a murderer was absolutely ridiculous. The more I thought about it, the more my muscles tensed.

Zeke walked up, carrying a bag from what I knew was his favorite sub shop, his face grim.

Alice led us through the living room, a space filled with

gorgeous houseplants and classy, neutral décor, and into her dining room. She gestured for us to sit, stepped into her kitchen, and returned with a notepad and pen. "Since John Harper seems to have lost his mind, we're going to have to figure this out," she said in a bitter tone. For a woman who was normally the picture of grace and decorum, this was the equivalent of screaming.

"Yeah." Zeke sat across from Alice, thumped down his giant to-go cup, and unwrapped his sub. He made a token gesture of offering some of the sandwich to Alice and me, then took an enormous bite.

I leaned in, both hands spread on the table. "We are definitely going to solve this. Because Detective Harper is wasting his time considering Cleo as a suspect when the killer—the real killer, who has murdered two people—is walking around scot-free." I forced myself to take a slow, calming breath. Now, more than ever, I needed to be logical. I needed to figure this out. If ever there was a time for persistence, this was it. "Let's look at the suspects. We need someone who would have had a motive to kill both Sheila and Carl."

"Which Detective Harper seems to be forgetting." Zeke's eyes blazed. "Two murders that close together? They have to be related. And there is no way—no way—Cleo would have killed Sheila."

"Lisa Brown, the woman with the leopard-print purse, seems unlikely. Being from out of town, she probably didn't know Sheila or Carl before the day of the auction." I explained how I had talked with her outside a restaurant downtown. "I believed her. And it's hard to imagine she would have found a reason to kill both of them."

Alice made a note on her pad. "Plus, Carl often walked on the bike path in the evenings. I knew that. Probably other people in Dogwood Springs did too. It's got some secluded spots that would be good locations if you wanted to kill someone. But how likely is someone from out of town to know about them? Or to know that Carl would be there?"

I thought for a moment. "It still seems to me that Danny would have wanted them both alive so the auction would go forward, and he would get his money. If, for some reason he did kill Sheila, killing Carl seems crazy. He's the auctioneer. Even if Jeannie could talk that fast, she seemed busy with the paperwork."

Zeke wadded up the wrapping from his sub. "And since Josh left, they're even more short-staffed. Plus, how's she going to hire someone? Who wants to work at a place where two people have been murdered?"

"My money's on Sandy. She could have killed both Sheila and Carl to keep the information about her ancestor owning those photos of scantily clad women a secret." I bit my lip. "I wish I'd been less trusting when I talked with her. That whole bit about going in early to unpack a shipment and working at the gift shop all day could have been a lie. I didn't even ask the assistant if it was true."

Alice patted my arm. "You can't blame yourself, Libby. And I do think Sandy is a good suspect, but—"

A knock sounded at the front door.

The three of us rushed to the entryway, and Alice pulled the door open.

"I'm here, finally." Cleo walked in and dropped her purse on the floor. Her hair was disheveled, her clothes were rumpled, and she looked exhausted.

Alice, Zeke, and I crowded around, all asking at the same time if she was all right, how she had found the body, and what the police had said.

Cleo put up two hands, palms out. "Hold on. I'll tell you the whole story."

Alice gestured for us to go into the dining room. "Let's sit. We were just trying to figure out who the real killer was since we know it wasn't you." She stopped at the door to the room. "Can I get you anything, Cleo?"

"Water. Maybe some saltines? My stomach is churning."

Alice disappeared into the kitchen and returned with a glass of ice water and a plate that held a stack of crackers and a piece of string cheese.

Cleo took a long drink of water and then let out a sigh. "Okay. To begin at the beginning, I thought that even though it was sticky, I should try to get some exercise. And I was wrong, but I'd hoped that the bike path was so shady that it would be cool. Anyway, I started at the far end, near the university, and was walking along, sweating and swilling sips from my water bottle, when I saw this lump on the sidewalk."

Zeke leaned in. "Carl's body?"

"It was, but at first, I didn't realize it. Then, when I figured out that it was a person, I thought they were hurt or maybe passed out from the heat. I ran up and"—she glanced away—"well, once I got close, it was clear he was dead. There was blood. Lots and lots of blood. And a big red spot on his chest, which is why I thought he'd been shot."

"He wasn't?" Alice said.

Cleo shook her head. "I heard one of the police officers say he was stabbed." She shuddered. "So, I called 911, and they sent an ambulance and the police, and the next thing you know, that idiot Detective Harper is asking me to come down to the station, saying that he'd heard how angry I was about Sheila's death." She pressed her lips together and her eyes narrowed. "Like I'm supposed to be happy about it. At that point, I called my dad." She looked over at Zeke. "I know I make fun of my dad and his cronies, but his buddy Lance Gilmore was at the station in less than ten minutes."

I must have looked confused because Alice tipped her head toward me. "Top criminal defense lawyer in town. Went to Harvard," she said quietly.

"Anyway, after I talked to Lance, things didn't take long. He read the detective the riot act about me simply being a good citizen by calling the police. Pointed out that if I'd killed Carl, the smart thing would have been to sneak off."

"Well, duh," Zeke said. "You'd think the detective could figure that out."

"So, I wasn't arrested, but I was told not to leave town." Cleo sagged into her chair. "And I sure hope we can find the real killer fast. What if all my clients cancel?"

"Goodness, that's never going to happen. They adore

you," Alice said. "But we do need to solve this case. And I think I have a valuable clue."

We all turned to look expectantly at her.

She ran a hand over her mouth, then set both hands on the table. "I hate to spread gossip, and I know this may upset you, Cleo, but I hear that Sheila was seen talking with Carl at that bar over on Welsh Street. Some people say they were having an affair."

"A bar on Welsh Street?" I wasn't even sure where that was.

"Behind the car dealerships. It's a townie bar, gets a few bikers," Zeke said offhandedly, as if, despite the fact that he was five years underage, he knew every bar in town.

Cleo gave him a pointed look and then turned to Alice. "I could see them meeting there, particularly if Sheila wanted to talk to him about the money he'd been skimming. That place is usually empty, so it would be a good place for a private conversation. But I can't in a million years see Sheila having an affair with Carl." She waved the idea aside. "Just ... no."

"It would give Jeannie an excellent motive to kill both of them," Alice said.

"It would also give Rick motive to kill both of them," I said slowly. "Sheila because she rejected him and Carl because of jealousy."

"I'm still not buying it." Cleo crossed her arms over her chest.

I glanced at Alice. Frankly, I agreed with her. Jeannie was the best suspect. But I'd need more than a feeling in my gut to convince Cleo or Detective Harper. "The best thing to do, I think, is gather more information. We can't trust anything anyone has told us. Everyone is back on the table."

Zeke raised one eyebrow. "Everyone?"

"Everyone," I said. "Lisa, Danny, Sandy, Jeannie, and Rick. We need to know where each of them was at the time of Carl's murder. Maybe some of them have a solid alibi, and that will narrow things down significantly."

Cleo angled her head to one side. "That does make sense."

Zeke and Alice both nodded.

I looked over at Cleo. "For now, I guess we should be grateful that Cleo's not in some jail cell, and we should let her go home and get some sleep. Tomorrow, we start digging deeper."

Chapter Seventeen

THE NEXT MORNING was such a whirlwind at the museum that I barely had time to think about the murders.

The public schools would be starting soon, teachers were back for a workday in their classrooms, and many were seeing Imani's emails about school tours for the first time, or at least deciding to respond to them. She was on the phone all morning, scheduling more tours and arranging to deliver various versions of our museum in a box, each a special collection of objects, documents, maps, and images related to a theme, perfect for a school lesson.

Plus, maybe partly because it was raining, four families from out of town came by, all of whom said they had been staying at local B & Bs and that the owners had suggested they visit. Three of the families were from the B & B owned by my mom's friend Faye Burke, but one was from another B & B, so clearly, our special outreach to the B & B owners was having an impact. I spent most of the morning answering questions from a ten-year-old girl who I expected to grow up to be a history professor.

At last, noon arrived, and I walked home in a thunderstorm. I ate some leftovers I found in my fridge, fed Bella, and let her out for a brief trip to the backyard. I dried her off and wiped the mud from her paws, then headed back to work.

I was only a few blocks from the museum when I spotted Sandy Byers leaving the gift shop. She had her purse over her shoulder and turned at the corner, as if she was headed to the lot where many downtown workers parked their cars.

I stopped on the corner, pretended to check a problem with my umbrella, and then looked at my phone, all while I watched her get into a large, blue SUV.

Then I scurried back down the block, skirted a big puddle where the sidewalk dipped, and slipped into the gift shop. If Sandy was gone, her assistant had to be running the place. It was too perfect an opportunity to pass up.

I left my dripping umbrella on a stand near the front door and found the assistant, a young woman with a narrow face and a nametag that said "Claire," looking bored and dusting the shelves near the miniature Dogwood Springs village buildings.

"Oh, I just love those," I gushed. In truth, I thought they were adorable, but I may have laid it on a little thick.

"Aren't they charming?" The woman's face brightened at the possibility of a sale. "This fall, we'll have a new building, the bookstore."

"I can't wait to see it." I hesitated, thinking through my lie. "I'm fairly new in town, and I came in recently, and Sandy showed me the little buildings. Let's see, it was a Saturday, a couple of weeks ago. The fifth." I looked at Claire, as if expecting her confirmation.

"The fifth of August? No, it couldn't have been then. Sandy was out all that day."

"Are you sure? I could swear it was the fifth."

"Normally, she is here on Saturdays, but that day, she asked me to keep the store by myself all day. She said she wasn't feeling well."

I forced myself not to do a dance of glee. My ruse had worked. If Sandy had really been ill that day, she would have told me so. Instead, she'd lied.

Which moved her to number one on my suspect list.

"Well, I guess I'd better get back to work. Thanks for telling me about the miniature bookstore. I'll be looking for it in the—"

"Libby, how nice of you to visit the shop again."

All thoughts of dancing drained from my body.

Sandy moved out from behind the end of the shelving unit, her lanky body tense, the lines around her eyes even deeper. "Claire, please go ahead and take your lunch break. I'll need lots of help this afternoon when we rearrange the card display."

Before I could think of a way to keep her around, the bell on the front door jingled as Claire slipped away.

"So, is there a reason you're checking up on me?" Sandy

eyed me up and down and reached toward a statue on a nearby shelf.

A statue made of brass—heavy, and perfect for a murder weapon.

My heart sped, and I glanced toward the door to the street. Could I escape?

A squeak drew my attention back to Sandy.

She had adjusted the statue, picked up the microfiber duster that Claire had left on the shelf, and was running it over the items.

I exhaled. Okay, maybe I was a bit on edge. Maybe she wasn't planning to kill me in the middle of her store. Still, I wanted an answer. "You have to admit that if someone was murdered on August fifth, and you lied about what you were doing that day, it does look suspicious." I stood up taller and tried to look fearless. "Suspicious enough that I probably should go to the police."

"I probably got confused." She flicked the duster across the next shelf down, gave me an unconvincing smile, and began dusting a collection of glass figurines.

I moved forward to a position where the heavy, brass statue was easy for me to grab. "It seems very unlikely that you'd get confused about what you were doing that day, the day that a woman was murdered, the same woman you'd argued with because you wanted your great-grandfather's collection of photos of half-dressed women kept secret."

Sandy set the duster on the shelf with a sharp click and turned to me, her eyes angry. "Fine. You want to know where I was?"

"I do." I wasn't backing down. Not with Cleo on the suspect list.

"Not that it's any of your business, but I was driving my son to a drug rehab center in St. Louis. He recently broke down and told his dad and me that he's got a real problem."

My stomach rolled like I'd eaten hotdogs laced with E. coli, and my cheeks grew hot. "Oh, I'm so sorry. Sorry I asked, and sorry about your son." I shifted my weight. "I hope, uh, I hope the rehab center can help."

"They say they can." She blinked rapidly, as if she was trying not to cry. "He was such a sweet little boy, and his dad and I—I mean, we weren't perfect parents—but we were decent. We tried. Family dinner almost every night. Went to all his school programs. Took him to church. And what if he gets clean and then starts doing drugs again?"

"It, uh, it sounds like you were great parents." I'd really stepped in it. Being nosy had led me into painful, personal matters that didn't have anything at all to do with the murder. And I didn't know what to say. I didn't know anything about being a parent and even less about addiction. "It, uh, it seems like a good thing that he came to you for help."

Sandy looked away, then turned back to face me. "That's what my husband says. He says all we can do is be supportive and hope for the best. He researched rehab centers and found a place that seems to have a great success rate."

"That sounds promising. I'm sorry I pried." I owed the

poor woman some explanation. "I'm worried because the police suspect my friend Cleo killed Carl Wilson."

"Cleo Anderson?"

I nodded.

"She'd never kill anyone." Sandy's voice rang with disbelief.

"I know. And it seems to me that both Sheila and Carl were murdered by the same person. If I can do anything to find the real killer and help Cleo, I feel I should."

"Well, it's not me." Sandy sniffed. "All I care about now is helping my son. Whatever stupid trash my great-grandfather collected is ancient history. I've got more important things to worry about than protecting his reputation, like making sure the store does well this summer. Rehab costs a fortune."

That made sense. And although I wasn't going to spread it all over town, realistically, even if she tried to keep her son's addiction a secret, people would find out. That seemed more likely to be a topic of gossip than sepia-tone photos of women hiding behind scarves or feather fans.

I apologized once again, picked up my umbrella, and stepped out onto the street. Then I hurried back to work, trying to stay dry despite the fact that the rain was now blowing sideways, and mentally crossing Sandy off the suspect list. What she'd revealed was too personal, and she'd seemed far too upset, for it all to have been a lie.

My list of possible murderers was down to four: Jeannie, Rick, Danny, and Lisa.

Chapter Eighteen

BY THE END of the workday, the rain had stopped. Gray clouds hung over Dogwood Springs, and the air was cool, almost fall-like, with much of the ragweed pollen settled to the ground. I walked home, carefully avoiding puddles and the big drips still running off the awnings downtown.

I spotted Bella's face at my living room window before I got to the sidewalk to the house. When I opened the door to my apartment, she wriggled out, her tail wagging.

"Hello, sweetie." I rubbed the soft fur on the top of her head. "Today is a perfect day for a long walk."

She let out a soft woof, trotted to the bedroom, and used her nose to push open the door of the closet where I kept my tennis shoes.

"Ready to go, huh?" I changed into shorts, put on my tennis shoes, and grabbed her leash from the hook near the kitchen door. After a quick stop in the backyard, I hooked it on, and we headed out on our longer path, down Elm Street toward Eighteenth, where we would cross the street and head back.

Bella and I weren't the only ones out enjoying the cooler temperatures. We saw my neighbor, Alan Melkins, a retired English professor who had taught at Grove University, a runner I didn't know, and two girls of about ten searching out puddles to stomp in with their boots.

The runner merely waved, but both the girls and Professor Melkins stopped to pet Bella and say hello.

And, luckily, the squirrel population appeared to be lying low until the rain dried. We didn't have a single barking incident the whole trip.

All in all, it was a delight. By the time we turned to head home, my worries about the murder had faded. Cleo, Alice, Zeke, and I would solve this case. Cleo's family would have closure. Things at the museum would improve. And Sam might even ask me out again.

Finally, we walked the last blocks toward home. We were about a block away when I saw Cleo's Jeep pulling into our driveway. I waved, but she didn't see me.

She must have gotten a call and sat in her car talking after she pulled in because she was just climbing out, still on the phone, when Bella and I reached the backyard.

"Love you too, Mom," she said, and she hung up.

I waved again.

"Libby, you're not going to believe this." Cleo came over to meet us. "My mom got a sympathy card in today's mail from a guy named Bill Peters. He lives in Westfield and wrote that he'd been dating Sheila for three months and that he was devastated to hear of her passing. He's made a donation to have a tree planted in her honor along the bike path."

Bella nudged Cleo's leg, and Cleo patted her head.

"You didn't know?"

"I had no idea, and neither did my mom. But from what the guy said in the card, they saw a lot of each other. I feel... I don't know..." She ran a hand over the back of her neck. "I feel almost hurt. I thought Sheila and I were so close. If I'd been seeing someone for three months, I'd have told her about him."

My chest tightened. "Maybe there was a reason she didn't tell you." Like maybe he was married. But I wasn't going to say that out loud. "This is a clue, Cleo, a really good clue. Because if this guy was dating Cleo and it was pretty serious..."

Cleo's eyes lit. "Then there was no way she was getting back with Rick, which means he lied to us."

I nodded. "And he might have been the one who killed her. I think we need to go talk to Bill Peters, to see what else he might know. If Sheila was spending a lot of time with him, he might know exactly why she was killed."

The next evening, I made a quick sandwich after work and gobbled it down while I looked at the website for the nursery owned by Bill Peters, which was located in the same town where Alice had grown up.

From what I could tell, the nursery was a large, successful venture. The website was slick, the photos were gorgeous, and the reviews were glowing. The business was open until eight, and, as I pointed out to Bella, it even had a paw print on the main page with a note that said shoppers were welcome to bring their dogs.

"Looks like you'll be coming with us, girl."

I waited until it was almost time to pick up Cleo before I mentioned the word *car* out loud.

As soon as I did, Bella was at the kitchen door.

"You'll have to ride in the back seat," I said as I grabbed my purse. "We're picking up Cleo."

Bella ignored me and walked up to the front passenger door. I was only able to get her to ride in the back when I unrolled her window. I might have imagined it, but I had a feeling that her former owner, Don, had lived a pretty solitary life and that Bella had ridden shotgun on almost every car trip.

As soon as I pulled in the parking lot at the salon, Cleo came out. She climbed in, said hello to Bella, and settled in, ready for the drive to Westfield.

The town, which was about the same size as Dogwood Springs, was about twenty miles up the highway, closer to St. Louis. The nursery, though, was well outside of town. All told, the trip took about half an hour.

"It looks nice, doesn't it?" Cleo glanced over at me, her eyes tense.

"It looks very nice. From what I could tell online, it

seems like a really successful business. I bet Alice has been here hundreds of times."

"She does have a bit of a plant addiction."

"As well as the greenest thumb I've ever known." I parked near the entrance of the main building, a metal structure surrounded by greenhouses, and looked at Cleo. "Ready to go in?"

"I guess. I still feel weird. Why did Sheila keep this guy a secret?"

"Let's ask him."

She made no movement to get out but sat there twisting a bracelet on her right arm. "Libby..."

"Not right off the bat, of course." I climbed out and opened Bella's door. "I'll be subtle."

Cleo let out a snort, which I ignored.

I clipped on Bella's leash, and the three of us walked into the metal building, where aisles of garden tools, flowerpots, and fertilizers were neatly arranged.

A young woman at the register told us that Bill was probably in Greenhouse No. 3, and we followed her directions out the back of the building.

Greenhouse No. 3 was filled with every color of chrysanthemum I'd ever seen, white and yellow and purple and pink and bronze and red.

Halfway down one side, a man of about fifty, wearing jeans and a red T-shirt sporting the nursery's logo, used a hose with a gentle dripping head to water the plants.

"Bill?" I said as we got closer.

"That's me." He turned, knelt to say hello to Bella, then stood and looked at us expectantly.

"I'm Libby Ballard and"—I gestured to my friend—"this is Cleo Anderson."

"Cleo! Sheila's favorite cousin!" He reached out and clasped her hands. "She loved you so much and spoke of you often. I'm very sorry for your loss." His brows drew together, and his eyes filled with sorrow.

"Thank you, uh, uh..." Cleo rocked from one foot to the other and glanced around. "Thank you for your card. My parents got it today."

He exhaled, and his expression eased a bit. "You're wondering why Sheila never mentioned me, aren't you?"

"Well..." Cleo looked down at her bracelet and twisted it again.

"We are," I said. "It seems from what you wrote that you and Sheila meant a lot to each other."

Bill closed his eyes for a moment and then nodded. "We did. I'd only been seeing her about three months, but I loved her. She was an amazing woman and very considerate about my situation."

A sick feeling rose from my stomach, and I tried to swallow it back. He was about to tell us he was married. I could just feel it.

"My ex-wife and I have been divorced for ten years, but when she got cancer, she didn't really have anyone else to lean on. If she thought I was seeing someone else, she'd have been uncomfortable asking as much of me as she did. So, I asked Sheila to keep things quiet. I wasn't in love with

Jacquelyn anymore, but I still cared for her, you know? And she needed me."

My breath whooshed out, and my stomach eased. He wasn't a cheater. He was a good man. And what did it say about me that I had expected the worst? Had I been burned so badly by my ex that I expected men to lie? Had one awful relationship ruined forever the way I would view the world?

"Anyway, my wife didn't have long to live, and Sheila was more than willing to keep our relationship secret so that Jacquelyn could have things as good as possible for her last days. A real fine woman, your cousin. I'm heartbroken that I won't get to see her again." He looked at Cleo. "I hope the idea for the tree was okay with your family."

Cleo's eyes shone. "It was." Her shoulders rose and fell as she let out a sigh. "And I appreciate you telling us about your ex-wife. It seemed odd that Sheila had kept you a secret, but now I understand." Her face softened. "I hope Jacquelyn is doing okay."

Bill looked away, then back at us. "Actually, she passed away just a few days before Sheila. I was at her funeral when I heard about the murder."

My heart twisted. The poor man. "How horrible."

"It was a blessing for Jacquelyn," he said. "What's horrible is that someone would kill Sheila."

"I couldn't agree more," Cleo said.

"That's, uh, that's partly why we're here." I tugged Bella back from a puddle she was sniffing. The water on the floor might have fertilizer in it, which couldn't be good for her.

"We wanted to ask you about Rick, her ex-husband. He told us that the two of them were getting back together."

Bill gave a harsh laugh. "Not a chance. He came to see Sheila as soon as he got back in town, and she told him to get lost. Frankly, I thought she should have reported him to the cops. He was pestering her nearly every day, bringing her these dumb little gifts, things she threw away as soon as he left."

I glanced over at Cleo. This put a whole different spin on the situation. Rick, who had seemed so nice, now sounded like a stalker.

"And Sheila knew he was drinking heavily again, back every night at his favorite bar from way back when, the Corner Pocket. She wanted nothing to do with him."

"All that rejection could make a man angry," I said. "Could possibly even make him commit murder. He sounds like someone we should talk to."

Bill's forehead furrowed. "It could. I certainly don't know of any other reason someone would have killed Sheila. But if he is the killer, you gals need to stay away from him."

Cleo gave me a pointed stare. "He's right, Libby."

"Okay, okay." I held up my hands, innocent as could be. "Bill, would you mind if we passed along what you said about Rick to the police?"

His brow relaxed. "Now that's a much better idea. I should have done that myself, except..."

Except the poor man had been dealing with a double dose of grief.

"We should let you go," Cleo said. "But I hope you'll be at the memorial service."

"I wouldn't miss it. I want a chance to say goodbye." He blinked and turned away, busying himself with watering.

We called out our goodbyes and walked to the car, leaving Bill to his grief.

"First thing tomorrow, we should call Detective Harper." Cleo latched her seatbelt. "Or do you think we should go by?"

I started the engine and backed out of the parking space, then glanced over at Cleo as I turned around to face forward. "What would you say to a little investigative work tonight, before we go to the cops?"

Chapter Nineteen

CLEO'S EYEBROWS SHOT UP. "Are you nuts? I am not going over to Rick's house and telling him we know he lied."

I shook my head. "That's not what I mean. I was thinking we should go to the Corner Pocket and see what the bartender knows. Like, if they heard Rick say something when he was drunk, like how he planned to kill Sheila or Carl, that would be even better evidence to take to the police."

"Don't you think if they'd heard that, they'd already have told the police?"

"Maybe. Maybe not." I explained about how reluctant Josh had been to talk to the police because of the run-in over spray paint. "I don't see how it can do any harm to ask."

"Well..." Cleo turned to look at Bella. "I don't think we can bring a dog into the Corner Pocket."

"We could drop her off at home. And it's not even seven. Still early."

Cleo raised her hands in surrender. "Fine. But if we walk in and Rick is there, drinking, we're going home. Immediately. Agreed?"

"Agreed." I might be eager for justice, but even I had no desire to tangle with a drunk man who might have already killed twice.

Later that evening, after Bella had lain down in front of my fireplace, happily gnawing a dog biscuit, and after Cleo had changed her outfit, we pulled up in front of the Corner Pocket.

I wrinkled my nose.

"I tried to talk you out of this," Cleo said. "This place is a dump."

She was right. The bar was a storefront in a weary strip mall that also featured a cheap nail salon, a bail bondsman, and a pawn shop. The asphalt parking lot was pitted with potholes, the neon sign over the bar read, "he Corn ocket," and, once we were inside, the dim interior smelled of stale sweat, spilled beer, and desperation.

Cleo and I glanced at each other and then scanned the room.

"I don't see Rick," she said.

"Me either." I pointed toward the bar. "Let's talk to her."

The woman behind the bar came toward us. "What can I get you?"

Cleo ordered Bud Light in a bottle, and I asked for a Diet

Coke. "And some information." I motioned for her to keep my change.

"I didn't think you all were here for the ambiance," the bartender said.

I wasn't sure how to respond.

She laughed. "Ah, I know this place is a dump. But I finally got the legal work finalized with my cheating ex, and it's all mine, as of today. I've got someone coming in the day after tomorrow to steam clean the carpet and redo the electrical, so I can put some brighter bulbs in here. I can't spend much, not after what my ex did to my finances, but at least this place can be clean and well-lit enough that I can see to kill the roaches."

"I'm Libby." I tapped my chest. "Recently divorced from someone cut from the same cloth."

"JoBeth," she said. "Sorry to hear about your ex. But glad you're shed of him. What do you need to know?"

The bar owner's dishwater blond hair was pulled up in a ponytail. She wore a denim skirt, a Corona Light T-shirt, and little makeup. Her eyes held a look that said she was not just innately intelligent but street-smart, too. She'd see right through me if I tried to be subtle.

"What can you tell us about Rick Dillon?" I eased onto one of the barstools. "Did he ever say anything that made you think he might have killed his ex-wife, Sheila?"

"Nah." JoBeth looked over at a server, seemed to read a hand signal, and filled three shot glasses with whiskey.

The server picked up a plate of loaded potato skins from

the kitchen, then came to the bar, moved the glasses to her tray, and hurried away.

"Rick would never have hurt Sheila." She pointed to a stool two down from Cleo. "I can't tell you how many nights he sat right there and moaned about how much he loved her."

Cleo leaned in closer. "Even after she rejected him?"

"Even after she rejected him." JoBeth gave a firm nod. "Now, he did come in all bent out of shape one day, claiming that he heard a rumor she was seeing her boss, Carl Wilson. I wouldn't have been surprised if Rick had killed Carl."

I sat down my glass. "Really?"

"Really. Except for the fact that I know from what I read in the paper that at the time of the murder, Rick was sitting on that same stool, eating an egg sandwich and washing it down with screwdrivers."

"Well, that blows that theory." Cleo took a drink of her beer.

"Sorry, ladies." JoBeth turned toward the door, to a group of guys dressed in cowboy boots, one of whom winked at her.

"Thanks anyway." I finished my Diet Coke, and Cleo and I walked outside.

Cleo took a long, deep breath. "Fresh air, at last. That steam cleaner can't come soon enough. And you were right, it was a good idea to come here."

"But we still don't know who the murderer is." I let out a groan. "We've ruled out Sandy and Rick completely. Lisa and Danny don't have motives. Our best suspect is Jeannie, who might have killed Sheila so she couldn't tell anyone that Carl was skimming money off each auction, but we don't know of any reason she would have killed her husband, especially now that we know he wasn't having an affair with Sheila."

Cleo climbed in, slammed her car door, and the two of us headed home.

I didn't have a single solid suspect I could take to Detective Harper. If Jeannie was the killer, she'd already lied to me once, without giving away a thing. The likelihood that I could talk with her again and make her slip up was slim. And I didn't have another direction to try.

Why couldn't I figure this case out? I'd done fine finding the person who killed my predecessor at the museum, someone I had no emotional connection to. But now, when the victim was Sheila, a woman I'd met and liked, a woman who meant the world to my best friend, I was a failure.

Chapter Twenty

THE NEXT MORNING, right after I hung up on a call where I confirmed the details for a presentation I was giving to the local Rotary club in September, the phone rang again.

It was the police.

My heart sped, but the call wasn't related to the murders. They had gone through the boxes I bought at the auction, Jeannie had confirmed that I had paid for them, and—because she had recently lost her husband—they were handling the transfer.

I had a noon meeting with a potential donor, so I arranged to pick them up as soon as I could get to the station after five.

An hour later, I got another call, this time from Sam.

"Hi, Libby. Am I catching you at a bad time?"

"No. This is fine." Pretty much any time he'd call was fine with me.

"I just got back in town last night, and I was wondering if you'd like to get together tonight to have dinner and look through those old school photos. Maybe we can figure out the name of the girl in the painting."

"Oh, I'd like that." I explained that I needed to let Bella out and had to pick up the boxes from the auction. "I'm rather excited to get them. They might contain treasure."

"Treasure?"

"Well, treasure to me." After I'd said it, I felt a little silly. I highly doubted that Sam would be excited about old dresses or shoes or hats or gloves. "I'm hoping for some historic clothing. But after those stops, I'm free."

"How about I pick up the boxes while you feed Bella? We can meet back at the museum, and I can transfer the boxes to your trunk or carry them inside, whichever you prefer."

"I couldn't ask you to do that."

"I'd be happy to. You know, I might be eager to learn that girl's name." He chuckled. "Or maybe to see you."

"Oh." Butterflies did some sort of modern dance number in my chest. "That would be wonderful. I'll let the police know you'll be coming by. See you in the museum parking lot at five thirty?"

"It's a date." Sam said goodbye and hung up.

Okay, to be honest, I didn't focus well the rest of the day. I'd try to work on a grant proposal and start wondering who killed Sheila and Carl. I'd tell myself to focus on the proposal budget and drift off into daydreams where the boxes were full of priceless historic clothing that had somehow survived decades unscathed. Or, despite the reservations in my head, my heart would win out, and I'd let out a sappy sigh and start thinking that I was about to go on my second date with Sam Collins.

Finally, at four thirty, I couldn't bear to look at the grant proposal any longer. Familiarizing myself with some of the museum's files could count as work.

I wouldn't look through the school photos without Sam, but I could definitely find them.

I shut down my computer and climbed the narrow stairs to the third-floor attic. Once I made my way through the doorway, I scanned the room. A worn worktable sat in the middle of the space, under the tallest part of the roof. Boxes and file cabinets filled the spaces under the eaves, and a bare-bones light fixture illuminated the space. I didn't wiggle past every box and check the very corners of the room, but at least, here in the middle, I didn't see a single spider or spider web.

Knowing Rodney, I should have expected things to be well-organized. With the index he had taped to the top of the first file cabinet, it took about two minutes to pull the folder with the photos from the Silersville School from the bottom drawer of the first cabinet. In later years, of course, a commercial photographer had taken school photos. But starting in 1901, shortly after the Eastman Kodak Brownie camera became available, a local businessman had purchased one and began a tradition of taking a photo of the teacher and students each year and having it framed and hung in the school.

I set the folder on top of the cabinet and resisted the urge to peek inside. That wouldn't be fair to Sam. I slid the drawer shut and took one more glance at the index. The museum was lucky to have Rodney. Hopefully, his recovery was going well, and he'd be back at work soon and—

Oh. There was a file on the Siler-Billington family. Cabinet three, second drawer down.

What kind of a historian would I be if I didn't flip through it? As I, of all people, should know, the answers to today's mysteries are sometimes hidden in the past.

I tugged it out of the drawer. The folder was a whopper, more than two inches thick, full of photos and newspaper articles and an amateur family history.

Five minutes later, I was back at my desk, flipping through the folder page by page, reading every detail. Some of the information I knew from the draft of the text Rodney had planned for the display about Jedidiah Siler. But Rodney only had room for the most important points, and all of it—the whole fabric of the lives of this family—was fascinating.

I settled deeper into my chair and kept reading.

A knock sounded at my door and startled me.

I dropped a newspaper clipping, which wafted its way to the floor.

"Sorry to startle you." Imani stood in the doorway. "I just wanted you to know I'm leaving, and you're alone here."

"Is it five already?" I picked up the clipping.

"Two past."

"Wow, did I lose track of time." I told her good night, left the Siler-Billington file on my desk, and hurried home to take care of Bella and get ready for my date.

Chapter Twenty-One

TWENTY-SEVEN MINUTES LATER, at exactly five thirty, I pulled into the lot behind the museum and parked.

Sam was already there, leaning against the side of his Tesla, looking incredibly handsome in a blue-and-white striped dress shirt and jeans.

I waved and climbed out of my car, then realized I'd forgotten my purse and reached back in for it. I popped back out and smiled at him. "Ready to do some historical detective work?"

"You bet." He walked toward me. "It's great to see you, Libby."

The modern-dance troupe of butterflies was back, performing another number in my chest. "It's, uh, it's great to see you too. Any problems at the police station?"

"None at all. Do you want to deal with the boxes first?"

"Why don't we do that later, when it's cooler?"

"Sounds smart to me."

I unlocked the back door of the museum, locked it behind us, and led Sam to the narrow steps to the attic. He had to stoop a bit going up, but once we were on the third floor, as long as he stayed near the center of the room, he could stand upright.

"Welcome to the storage room." I flipped on the lights and waved a hand around, taking what I hoped looked like a casual glance at the space. I had no real desire to let Sam know I was nervously scanning the room for spiders.

Unless, of course, one appeared.

Then I would gladly let him kill it.

"The school folder we want is right over here." I pointed to the file cabinet. "I checked earlier, to make sure we had it, but I didn't peek. And, of course, once we know her last name, we may want to check the files to see if we have more information on her family."

"You have information on old families?"

"Some of them, yeah."

His eyes gleamed. "Well, let's check those school photos!" He pulled out his phone. "I took a picture of the painting, so we'd be sure we found the right girl."

I gestured to the worktable in the center of the room, and we sat, side by side, with the folder on the table in front of us. "The painting was your discovery, so you go ahead."

He leaned in and opened the folder.

Inside, the top photo was labeled in a spidery hand as "The Silersville School—1901." One corner was ripped, and the photo had yellowed, but it clearly showed a serious-looking teacher, recognizable by the way she stood at one side, wearing slightly nicer clothes, and fifteen students, ranging in age from a girl of about seven to a boy who looked older than the teacher. Half of the children were barefoot, and many looked like they were wearing hand-me-downs. On the back, the same spidery hand identified the teacher as Isadora Watkins and listed the students and their ages.

"I think, based on the clothing, that the painting was done not long after 1900."

"I don't see our girl." Sam began to move the photo aside.

"Wait." I pointed to one girl in the photo. "Doesn't that look sort of like the girl in the painting?"

Sam studied the image more closely. "It does. It may be her but a couple of years before the painting was done." He quickly flipped through more photos, found one from 1903, and tapped a face with his finger. "Her."

I looked at the picture on his phone and then at the school photo. Except for the pose, the girls were identical. Even the hairstyle was the same. "It's her. It has to be."

He turned the photo over and ran a finger through the names. "Here. Ivy Whitfield, age sixteen." A slow smile spread over his face, as though he couldn't quite believe it.

Excitement rippled through my system, and I grinned in return. "We've done it! We've figured out the identity of the girl who was painted out of the portrait."

"And if you have information about her family, maybe we can find out why."

"C'mon." I stood and led the way to the file cabinets,

pointing to the paper taped to the top. "Let's check the index."

"I don't see Whitfield listed," Sam said. "Do you think it's under another name?"

I leaned down to study the index, and my shoulders sank. "No. Rodney's organized family information by the oldest ancestor's name, with lots of cross references for intermarriage. I guess the Whitfields aren't one of the families we have a file on. We may have to do a lot more digging online if we want to learn more."

"Hmmm. That sounds like something we might want to pursue another day. I don't think I've got the strength for online digging without dinner." Sam's eyes twinkled.

"I am getting hungry. And we did learn her name. Ivy Whitfield." I walked toward the doorway and shut off the lights. "Don't worry, Ivy, we'll figure out what happened to you one day."

Sam led the way down the narrow staircase but stopped once we were on the second floor. "So, did you want me to carry the boxes from the auction into the museum, or do you want to take them home?"

"If they're full of junk, the museum has a big dumpster. Inside, I guess."

"Okay, so, you can totally say this is a bad idea, but you had me interested when you mentioned that they might contain 'treasure.' What if we go get some dinner, and then I can carry them in for you and stay to see what you find?"

"That would be fine with me, but I have to warn you,

those boxes are probably full of worn, ugly clothes from the 1970s."

"Still, they might have treasure." Sam covered one eye with his hand, as if it were a patch. "Aaar!"

I giggled. "Fine, let's go get dinner, Pirate Sam."

After dinner, Sam and I were so full that we decided to walk to my apartment, get Bella, and bring her back to the museum with us.

I opened the door to my apartment, only to be nearly knocked down as my dog rushed out to welcome Sam. "Bella, calm down."

"No, no, it's fine." Sam knelt to pet Bella, laughing out loud when she licked his cheek.

She flopped down on the floor beside him, and when he rubbed her belly, she rolled back and forth in utter bliss.

If I didn't know better, I'd say she loved Sam more than me.

As for me, well, the more time I spent with Sam, the more I liked him. Over dinner, I'd updated him on the investigation into Sheila's death. As we discussed things, he'd made connections so quickly that it was no wonder he'd made a fortune in tech. Add in his goofy sense of humor and good looks, and my personal vow to protect my heart was weakening.

Eventually, when Bella allowed Sam to stand, we walked back to the museum, and he carried in the three boxes I'd bought at the auction, arranging them on the conference room table. No need to haul them upstairs if they all might be trash.

"Time to hunt for treasure," he said as he sat the last box on the table.

I dug a pair of scissors out of the drawer under the coffee maker and carefully cut open the first box.

Sam lifted the flaps.

Even Bella stood by, peering at the box.

What we found inside could not by any stretch of the definition be considered treasure. It was not historic clothing. Not even vintage clothing. More like clothing that, twenty or thirty years ago, had been cheap to begin with, worn frequently, and put away without laundering.

Sam and I looked at each other.

"No treasure yet," he said.

"Nope." The second box was no better. Still hopeful, I carefully cut the tape on the third box. Inside, I found children's clothes that looked like they might have been from the 1960s. But except for a pink dress that might have been worn by a flower girl, they hadn't held up well. I set them on the table and picked up an item packed in tissue paper.

Bella sniffed at the flower girl dress.

Doggy drool would not help that delicate, old fabric. I gently pushed her head away, unwrapped the tissue paper, and squealed.

Sam moved closer. "What have you found?"

"A purse!" I held up a bag with a Bakelite handle. "Definitely vintage and possibly worth a good deal of money to a collector."

"People collect old purses?" His tone implied that this was one step above collecting dryer lint.

"You'd better believe it." I peered down into the box at bundle after bundle wrapped in tissue.

One by one, I unwrapped them, oohing and ahhing over almost every one. I found vintage designer bags by Gucci and Hermès and several by Chanel. There was no way Sheila had packed this box for the auction. I felt sure she would have recognized their value. But Josh might not have. Which had turned out very nicely for me.

In the very bottom of the box, I found one purse that, had it been me, I wouldn't have kept. It was a rather boring vinyl bag, special only because it was bright red.

I set it aside and held up one of the Chanel bags. "I might just have to keep this one for myself. For special occasions, you know." I slid the chain and leather strap over my shoulder and pirouetted.

Sam chuckled, then stopped. "Hey, Bella, no."

I looked back.

She'd grabbed the red vinyl bag in her mouth, opened the flap, and was twisting the purse back and forth.

"Bella, no!" I took hold of the purse. "Give. Now."

She gave me a look that said this was all a game to her and shook the purse again.

"Bella!"

Another look, this time one I couldn't interpret. She dropped the purse at my feet.

"I bet it's got tooth marks all over it," I said. "I mean, I don't think this one was valuable, but still, I didn't want her to—"

I froze, pointing at some paper that was peeking out where Bella had ripped the lining.

I wriggled the paper out from behind the lining and found that inside the purse, someone had hidden not just one, but three letters.

Sam and I looked at each other, and then we each picked up a letter.

Chapter Twenty-Two

I OPENED the envelope in my hand. "It's a love letter. To Marjorie Billington." I flipped it over and read the bottom of the page. "From Tobias Brown."

"This one too," Sam said.

Sam and I stared at Bella.

She gave us her typical doggie smile, but her eyes gleamed especially bright. There was no way she could have known the letters were hidden inside the lining of the purse, was there?

No, it had to be a coincidence.

I carefully opened the third letter, and Sam rearranged them, putting them in order by date with the first letter that had been sent on top.

I gestured to the table, and we sat, side by side, with the stack of letters on the table between us.

Quickly, I read through the first letter, dated November 12, 1964. Reading between the lines, it was clear that Tobias and Marjorie had met when she contacted him about restoring the armoire. The attraction between them had been instantaneous, and while Marjorie's husband was away in the Vietnam War, she and Tobias, who had not been drafted because he had diabetes, had an affair. The letter was written in a neat, narrow hand and ran almost the full front and back of the paper.

"He wanted her to leave her husband," I said.

Sam nodded.

I moved the first letter to the back of the stack, and we started the second letter.

Marjorie, apparently, had said no. Her husband was wealthy, and Tobias was not. If she left her husband, it would affect not only her life but also her parents' lives. The scandal of her having an affair while her husband was away serving his country, plus the loss of financial support from her husband, would destroy them. The letter didn't say it outright, but it seemed as if her whole reason for marrying had been the Billington money. Still, Tobias pleaded, writing that although he couldn't give her the finer things in life, he made a decent living. "The two of us could be so happy together," he promised.

The third letter was much shorter than the last two. We leaned in to read the tight script.

Dearest Marjorie,

I beg of you to reconsider.

I understand that you feel, since your husband has been wounded, that people might judge you and your family more harshly if you leave him, but some things are far more impor-

tant than social standing. I know you say your parents would be destitute without your husband's money, but you know that's not the case. They simply would no longer be seen as one of the wealthiest families in town.

Think of your happiness. Of my happiness. Of the many children we could have together. As you've told me, if you stay with Charles, you will never hold your own baby in your arms.

I will always, always love you. I will keep my promises to you, and I treasure everything we had together. But, unless you reply, this will be the last time I contact you. I do not want to make your decision any harder than it must already be.

Please reconsider, my darling.

Tobias

"Man." Sam leaned back in his chair. "I wonder what he promised her?"

"Probably to never breathe a word of their affair." I laid a hand on the stack of letters. "It's just so sad. Deep down, Marjorie must have regretted her decision. Otherwise, why would she have kept the letters?"

"Do you know when her husband died?"

"I don't remember, but I can find out. Just a minute." I ran upstairs to my office, where I'd left the Siler-Billington family file, and brought it back. "I was reading through this, thinking I might find some clue that would explain the murders. I haven't found that, but I think the obituary for Charles is in here."

We flipped through the folder and, after a few minutes, found the newspaper clipping.

Sam brushed away a bit of paper that had flaked off another document and pointed to the date. "1972. It asks for donations to the American Heart Association, so he probably had a heart attack."

We repacked the boxes, and Sam carried two to the dumpster and loaded the third into my trunk. I stuck the letters and the Siler-Billington file in my big purse. Now that I'd started learning about the family, I wanted to know more.

At last, with everything packed up, Bella lounging in my front passenger seat, and the museum locked, I leaned against my car. "I wonder why Marjorie didn't marry Tobias after her husband died. She would have inherited his money, and if she and Tobias had waited a year, I can't see how anyone could find that scandalous."

Sam shrugged. "Maybe by that time, Tobias had married someone else."

"Poor Marjorie. And she never remarried. She lived here all alone for years. Very sad."

"Yep. She gave up love and happiness for money and social standing. That seems like a very bad trade."

I looked over at him. "You sound like a romantic."

"Nah. I'm tough." He crossed his arms over his chest and put on a stern expression. But he could only hold it for a second before the corners of his lips twitched.

"Right." I laughed. "And you kick puppies and evict orphans."

His mouth gaped. "Well, no! What kind of person do you think I am?"

"I think," I said, running a finger down his arm, "that you're a big softie."

"Maybe." He stepped closer and wrapped one arm around my waist. "But don't tell anyone."

"It will be our secret." I slid my hands around the back of his neck.

A slow smile spread across his face. "You know, we probably should seal that deal," he said, leaning toward me.

My heart pounded, and I nodded.

And I closed my eyes as he kissed me.

The next morning, I overslept. I drove to work and managed to get there only half an hour late but didn't have enough time, either before work or once I got to the museum, to even send a text to Cleo, Alice, and Zeke to tell them what Sam and I had learned.

At lunch, I drove home, promising myself that I would text them while I ate a quick sandwich.

Cleo was leaving as I arrived.

"Hey," I called out as she walked toward the garage. "Are you just going into work?"

"I am. I had a dentist appointment this morning. Not an easy one." She cupped her jaw. "I'm still numb, and I bit my tongue eating lunch."

"Ouch." I met her in front of the garage and patted her arm. "I'm sorry. Maybe some ice cream would help."

"Good idea." She raised the garage door.

"But I'm glad I saw you. I was going to text you." Quickly, so I wouldn't make her late for her first appointment, I told her about the letters.

"An affair, huh? From what I heard about Marjorie's parents, I bet that would have killed them. They were very proper, very focused on having dinner with only the 'right couples.'" She pulled out her phone. "Got to run. One of my clients has her daughter visiting from Nebraska. The two of them look almost like twins, and the daughter wants her hair highlighted just like her mom's before she goes home."

I backed away and waved, then hurried to my kitchen door. I needed to get back to work to meet with a man who was interested in donating to the museum.

Bella wriggled out the instant the door cracked, ready for attention, a quick gallop around the backyard, and a roll in the grass. I sat on the steps, mentally reviewing the contents of my fridge and deciding on a fried egg sandwich. It was fast and—

Wait a minute. Cleo's comment about the mother and daughter who looked so much alike made me think of something.

"Bella, let's go in."

She twisted from side to side, all four feet up in the air, as if scratching her back on the grass.

"Bella, c'mon!"

She rolled over and trotted toward me.

I hustled her inside and sat down on the couch by the Siler-Billington folder. Less than a minute later, I found it.

A photo of Marjorie Billington from years ago. A photo

that, now that I studied it more closely, looked an awful lot like Lisa Brown.

I sat back on the couch and stared at the photo. If I hadn't been so starry-eyed over Sam last night, I would have put it all together sooner.

I hurriedly sent a text to Cleo, Alice, and Zeke, along with photos of the letters, and asked them to meet me at my apartment at seven, when Cleo got off work.

"I think I know who killed Sheila," I said to Bella.

She tipped her head toward me.

"Danny." As I prepared to go meet the potential donor, I explained to Bella about the letters. "I've got a whole new theory about why this murder was committed."

Chapter Twenty-Three

AT SIX THIRTY, Alice texted. She'd gotten behind and had yet another cake still in the oven. Could we meet at her place instead of mine? She even invited Bella and said we could sit on her patio.

Half an hour later, I led Bella around to the back of Alice's house.

Zeke and Cleo were already there, sitting at a round table on the deck under a big red umbrella.

Bella walked up to each person, making sure they all had a chance to pet her.

Once she'd gotten some attention, I offered her a dog treat, and she flopped down on the deck near my feet.

"You went to my favorite sub shop, and you didn't get me anything?" Zeke gave Cleo a wounded look as she unwrapped a six-inch grilled veggie sub.

Cleo shrugged at him. "I know for a fact that your mom

made spaghetti and meatballs tonight. Didn't you already eat?"

"Well, yeah, but I always have room for more." He slid his fingers toward her potato chip bag.

She slapped his hand away. "Mine. I barely ate any lunch. Now that the Novocain has worn off, I'm starving."

Alice rolled her eyes. "You two are worse than my kids when they were little. Zeke, do you want me to make you a sandwich? I've got leftover roast beef."

Bella's ears perked up.

But Zeke brushed the offer aside. "Nah."

Alice peered over at him. "Are you sure?"

"I'm sure."

"Okay." She looked as if she didn't really believe him but turned to me. "Libby, what's the news? Who do you think the killer is?"

I leaned forward with both hands on the table. "Danny."

"Danny?" Zeke tipped his head to one side. "Why?"

"Last night, Sam helped me carry the boxes of clothes I bought at the auction into the museum."

"He did?" Cleo raised her eyebrows at Alice. "Sounds very promising, don't you think?"

I ignored her and tried to shift the conversation. "Zeke, did you ever contact him about studying computer science in college?"

Alice mirrored Cleo's raised eyebrows and nodded at her. "Carrying in boxes sounds very promising."

Zeke looked from Alice to Cleo and back again, then

glanced over at me and mumbled that he would call Sam eventually.

Alice laid a hand on my arm. "When are you seeing Sam again, Libby?"

"We—" Hold it. "That's not the point. The point is that one of the boxes was full of these incredible vintage purses..." I paused for effect and saw both Cleo and Alice sit up taller. "And thanks to Bella, who grabbed one of the purses and ripped the lining, we learned that it hid letters that Tobias Brown, a man who used to run a woodworking shop here in town, had written to Marjorie Billington. The two of them had an affair while her husband was away during the Vietnam War."

"Good job finding a clue, Bella," Zeke said.

She stood and gazed up at him with adoring eyes.

He petted her and told her she was smarter than most humans he knew.

"You told me that much when I saw you at lunchtime," Cleo said. "And you texted us the pictures of the letters. That doesn't explain why you think Danny was the killer."

"It will when I tell you that Lisa told me she was raised only by her father because her mother had died when she was a baby. And Marjorie had contacted her not long before she died and wanted Lisa to come visit her to give her the armoire that her father had repaired. Plus Lisa looks really similar to an old photo of Marjorie that I found from when she was the age Lisa is now. And listen to this."

I pulled my phone and read part of one of the letters aloud.

"Okay." Zeke scrunched up his nose. "They had an affair and Marjorie stayed with her husband because he was rich and because she didn't want to freak out her parents."

"So," I said, moving my foot out from under Bella's head. She'd laid back down and was drooling on my sandal. "Think about those phrases he used. 'Some things are far more important than social standing ... the many children we could have together ... you'll never hold your own baby in your arms.'"

Alice's face fell. "Oh my."

"What?" Zeke said.

"What if Lisa's mother really wasn't dead? What if the promise Tobias made to Marjorie was that he would raise their daughter, Lisa, but never tell anyone who the mother of the child was? What if Danny killed Sheila because she found some other paper that Marjorie had hidden away, like a birth certificate, that would prove to everyone that Lisa was Marjorie's daughter? Lisa would be a much closer relative than Danny, and that would put his inheritance in question."

Zeke's forehead scrunched up. "Wouldn't everyone know Marjorie had a baby? It would have been hard to hide when she was really pregnant."

"Back then," Alice said, "fewer women worked outside the home. Marjorie could have simply told people she was lonely with her husband away at war and gone to stay with a sister or cousin or friend out of town for a few months and had the baby there."

Understanding flickered in Zeke's eyes. "Can we look up

Lisa Brown's birth certificate online? So we could prove that Marjorie and Tobias were her parents?"

"No. I think, to avoid things like identity theft, they're kept private."

Zeke's eyes narrowed. "Maybe I could hack my way in."

Cleo punched him in the arm. "Hack into state records? Don't even think about it."

"Detective Harper could get access," I said quickly. I certainly didn't want Zeke to do anything illegal. "I'm taking him these letters first thing tomorrow morning. I think this, combined with the fact that Rick saw Danny arguing with Sheila and that Danny made no secret that he needed money, should be enough to convince the detective to take a long, hard look at Danny."

Cleo ran a hand through her hair. "If this is true, when Marjorie asked Lisa to come to see her, she really just wanted a chance to meet her before she died, didn't she?"

"I think so. It seems like later in life, she regretted her choice."

Alice's forehead creased. "I guess we can't know how much pressure her parents put on her. Or if she later wanted to contact her daughter but thought she wouldn't want anything to do with her."

"You may be right." Cleo dug into her potato chip bag, tipped her head back, and dropped the last crumbs into her mouth. "Maybe, when she learned she was dying from cancer, she decided to take the chance."

We chatted a little longer, and then Zeke, Cleo, Bella, and I headed home. Once Cleo and I got back to Elm Street, she went up the back stairs to her apartment, but I stayed outside to allow Bella some time in the yard.

She galloped over to her favorite tree, and I sat down on my back stoop. Fireflies danced in the dim evening light, and leaves rustled in the light breeze.

When I first moved to Dogwood Springs, I had feared that living here might be boring. I had underestimated the town, which offered more amenities than I'd expected, but I'd also underestimated the joy of simple pleasures like spending a quiet moment on my back stoop. In Philly, I'd never really taken time for such things.

My quiet moment was short lived, though. After a quick trip to a tree across the yard, Bella started back toward me and then froze, her nose twitching. She raced to my side, growled, and barked loudly at my back door.

Chapter Twenty-Four

COLD SWEAT BROKE out all over my body.

The screen door above me banged open. "What's going on?" Cleo thudded down the stairs.

I pointed to my back door. "I don't know. I think Bella's trying to warn me that someone's been inside. Or maybe is still in there. Should we call the cops? But what would I say? My dog barked?"

"We should check to see if there really is a problem." Cleo stood up taller. "Remember all those self-defense classes I told you I took? Now's the time to use them. You stay in the back and let Bella and me go in first."

I nodded and dug into the depths of my purse, pulling out my pepper spray, a relic of my life in Philadelphia. With it in one hand and my key in the other, I started to unlock the door.

But it fell open, already unlocked.

My hands dropped to my sides, suddenly clammy, and a rock seemed to have formed in my stomach. Even from the doorway, I could tell someone had been in my apartment.

Kitchen drawers hung open, and my laptop, which I was almost certain I'd left on the end of the counter, was gone.

Bella lunged in, barking loudly.

"Bella, no. Come here!" My heart pounded as I shoved my keys in my purse, scrambled to grab her collar, and yanked her back outside.

"We'd better go upstairs," Cleo said. "No one had been there."

I agreed, and she hurried up the outside stairs.

I followed more slowly, pulling on Bella's collar. She came with me but continued barking, occasionally tugging away from me and letting out a growl.

Upstairs—just to be sure—we searched Cleo's apartment, but we found no intruders.

Cleo made sure both doors were locked tight, dug a baseball bat out of her bedroom closet, and sank into her vivid blue armchair.

I collapsed onto her couch. My hands trembled as I pulled my phone from my purse and dialed the police.

Then I called Bella over, hugged her, and thanked her for warning me.

Ten minutes later, Tate and another uniformed officer arrived, followed shortly by Detective Harper. He made sure we were unharmed, then sent the officers to check my apartment and asked Cleo if there was somewhere we could sit down.

She led the way to her living room, waved him toward the armchair, and sat with me on the couch.

Bella sat on the floor beside me, her head against my leg, as if she understood how much comfort it gave me to have her nearby.

"Libby, Cleo." He nodded to each of us and said hello to Bella. His salt-and-pepper buzz cut looked even shorter than the last time I'd seen him. "Tell me what happened." He pulled a small notepad from the pocket of his blue dress shirt and rested it on his knee, where the cover blended in perfectly with his black pants.

We explained that we had been at Alice's.

"I left here about six thirty," I said. "And everything was fine."

"And we got back before nine," Cleo added.

"But Bella knew something was wrong." I told him how she'd barked and come to guard me.

He glanced at Bella, then looked back at me. "We'll have you go through your apartment, Libby, to see what's missing. Did you notice anything when you went in?"

"I think my laptop is gone. I guess I could have put it somewhere else, but I try to leave it on the kitchen counter."

"I had a glimpse in her living room," Cleo added. "Her TV is definitely gone."

"Uh-huh." The detective rubbed the back of his neck.

"Stuff that's high value, easy to unload. Sounds like the same burglar who was hitting the businesses downtown. It's been more than a week since the last break-in. I had almost decided the criminal had moved on."

"But except for Sheila's house, I thought all the thefts were at businesses downtown," I said.

"Before this, they were." Detective Harper frowned. "I guess, since we were having extra patrols downtown, they switched to private homes."

"Why would they pick my house?" It really didn't seem fair. Or logical. There were certainly places where they could find a lot more things of value.

Footsteps thudded up the stairs at the front of the house, and someone knocked on Cleo's front door.

The detective opened it, admitting Officer Tate.

"No one downstairs, sir. It looks like they picked the lock on the back door to gain access."

I glanced over at Cleo. How were we supposed to feel safe here?

The detective stood. "Let's go downstairs, Libby. Try to determine what's been taken, but don't touch anything. Bella, you stay here with Cleo."

Downstairs, I stopped briefly in the living room. As Cleo had said, the TV was gone, one end of the cable cord still plugged into the wall, the other flung over the antique dresser I used as a TV stand. The stereo and my collection of '70s albums were undisturbed, but my laptop was nowhere to be seen.

For the life of me, I couldn't remember what the deductible was on my renter's insurance. At least the documents and photos on my laptop were backed up in the cloud. Other than my antique furniture, which didn't seem to have interested the thief, the only thing I had of value was some jewelry. Thankfully, my pearls were being repaired, and the vintage purses were still in my trunk.

I exhaled a shaky breath and turned toward the bedroom. "I almost don't want to look."

The detective angled his head slightly, his eyes sympathetic.

I steeled myself and walked in.

My heart sank.

The wooden jewelry box sat open, the velvet-lined compartment where I always carefully stored my good jewelry, empty.

"My emerald earrings are gone. The ones my parents gave me when I graduated college." Darn it, I didn't have much nice jewelry, especially since I'd sold everything my ex had given me. But those earrings meant a lot to me.

"I'm sorry, Libby." Detective Harper stepped closer. "Do you have photos of them? We can check the local pawn shops."

"I do. And a pearl ring is gone. It's an antique. I have a photo of it too." I'd been so excited when I found it at an estate sale about five years ago. Somewhere, in the thousands of photos on my phone, there was a shot that I had sent my ex-husband after I bought it.

I stepped back from the dresser and scanned the room. Drawers were open, but nothing else appeared to have been taken. As if the burglar had done this many times and knew how to take the most valuable stuff in as little time as possible.

"Sir?" Officer Tate called from my kitchen door. "We may have found footprints. Can you come take a look?"

"Keep looking around, Libby," Detective Harper said. "I'll be right outside."

"Okay." I went back out into the living room, then paused. Something wasn't right. Something else was gone. I closed my eyes and tried to picture the room before I'd left for Alice's.

"Oh!" I raised a hand to my chest and opened my eyes.

I was right.

I hurried outside to Detective Harper and Officer Tate, careful to only walk on the sidewalk. "They're gone," I said.

Detective Harper turned to me. "What's gone?"

"The letters I found in a purse I bought at the Billington auction. The ones I was going to bring you tomorrow."

The more I thought about it, the more my stomach tightened. Being a random victim of crime was unnerving. Being targeted because of my investigation? Much, much worse.

Detective Harper pulled out his notepad. "Tell me about these letters."

I explained how I'd bought the boxes of clothing and found the three letters. "I think they help explain Danny's motive. I bet if you call the state and get Lisa Brown's birth certificate—I've got her number so you can call and get her birthday to make sure you find the right Lisa Brown—you'll find that Marjorie is her mother. And if Sheila found something like a birth certificate that proved that, it could mean that Danny didn't inherit."

Detective Harper's jaw tightened.

"Rick Dillon overheard Danny arguing with Sheila the morning she was killed. And I heard Danny pressuring Jeannie to reschedule the auction quickly so he would get his money. I really think it all makes sense. Don't you see?"

His jaw became rigid. "All I see is that you've been interfering with an ongoing murder investigation. I strongly doubt that this burglary had anything to do with the two murders, but if it did, you've gotten yourself right in the middle of the murderer's radar."

"But—"

"But nothing." The word "stern" was about three levels of magnitude too mild for his tone. "I need you to grab a few things and stay upstairs with Cleo or with another friend or at a hotel tonight. We'll finish gathering evidence tomorrow."

I bit my lips together, forcing myself not to contradict him. Deep down, I knew he was right. I had been interfering. But he wasn't listening to the very clear evidence I was presenting. Or maybe it wasn't that clear. Maybe I was too keyed up to make my points well.

"And for heaven's sake"—he glared at me—"stop trying to solve the murders."

Fine. For tonight, I'd leave things alone. Tomorrow, when I wasn't so upset, I'd go see him in his office. If I presented my points slowly and logically, I was sure I could get him to request a copy of Lisa Brown's birth certificate.

Chapter Twenty-Five

THE NEXT MORNING before I went to work, I called the police station and, after looking at my calendar, made an appointment to see Detective Harper at four o'clock.

My day was packed with out-of-the-office meetings, including driving to Jefferson City to have lunch with a major donor. Despite the unease that crept up when I thought about the break-in at my apartment, the day sped by. My three o'clock called to cancel, though, and I returned to the museum, hoping to sit in my quiet office and soak up the air-conditioning.

I had just turned my car engine off when my phone rang. I'd snagged a spot in the shade, so for a few minutes at least, my car would be comfortable. I dug the phone out of my purse, answered, and put it on speaker. "Hey, Cleo, what's up?"

"Sheila's best friend, Adelaide, called me back. You're never going to believe what she told me."

I set the phone on the console. "Well, don't keep me in suspense."

"You were close with your theory that Sheila may have found Lisa Brown's birth certificate. But what Sheila actually found was a will where Marjorie left everything to her illegitimate daughter."

That didn't make sense. "Wouldn't her lawyer have a copy of the new will? Wouldn't Danny already have known that he didn't inherit?"

"No, this was a will she wrote herself the night before she died. Sheila told Adelaide that she found it behind the nightstand when she was staging the room for the auction. She thinks maybe Marjorie put it on the nightstand, and it got knocked off."

"Does a will like that even hold up in court?"

"That's how come Adelaide knows about it. She's a lawyer. Sheila texted her a photo of the will and asked if it was valid."

"And?"

"Apparently, it depends what state you're in. Adelaide said Marjorie must have looked it up online because Missouri requires that if you write out your own will by hand and sign it, you also need two witnesses to sign it, and Marjorie got two signatures. Adelaide recognized the names. She says one is a home health aide, and the other does yard work."

I sat for a minute, thinking and getting hotter by the second. Finally, I turned the car back on long enough to open both front windows, so I got some breeze. "I wonder why neither of the witnesses told the police about this."

"Hmmm." I heard a *snick, snick, snick* sound come over the phone line, as if Cleo was clicking the end of a ballpoint pen. "You know, the witnesses might not have any idea who's inheriting Marjorie's estate. Or"—she drew in a breath—"this makes more sense. She might not have shown them the whole will. She might have covered up everything except where she had them sign. I've seen people do that on TV."

"You're right. If Sheila found that will and Danny knew about it, it definitely makes sense that he would kill her. If she told Carl about it, that gives Danny a reason to kill him too. And if Danny was the one who broke into Sheila's house, he could have stolen the will and burned it."

"Yeah, but Adelaide has the phone message with the photo. And she thinks it can be proven to be acceptable in court."

"Did she send you the photo?"

"She did. I'll forward it to you."

"Thanks. I've already got an appointment to see Detective Harper in a couple of hours. I think with this, he'll finally listen to me."

"I should hope so," Cleo said. "Oh, got to go, I don't want to leave the color on my client too long." She hung up.

I turned my car back on long enough to roll up the windows and got out.

Four o'clock couldn't come soon enough. I couldn't wait

to see Detective Harper's face when I explained how I had cracked the case.

Sheila's murder would be solved, all suspicion would be removed from Cleo, and Danny Larsen would be in custody by nightfall.

As soon as I walked in, Imani asked me if I could man the front desk and watch for visitors. She had several versions of our museum in a box, all ready to deliver. She promised to be back before four so I could go to my meeting with the detective.

Once again, she said, the museum was empty, but both of us had gotten more optimistic over the past few days. With luck, someone would come in.

She picked up the last three boxes and headed out the back to her car.

I strolled through the displays on the first floor, my flats clicking against the hardwood floors. There was additional display space upstairs, but I had checked it earlier. I straightened the easel where we had an announcement about the birthday party and took a seat at the front desk. If a visitor arrived, we were ready.

A second later, my phone rang.

It was Sam.

I quickly picked up.

"Hi, Libby. I talked to the appraisers. They say they can

easily have the painting back before the town birthday party."

Excitement bubbled up inside me. "Really?" I walked to the conference room, where I'd stashed a bottle of soda in the fridge. "Oh, Sam, that's wonderful. Thank you." I took a drink and stuck the bottle back in the fridge.

The bell on the front door jangled as a visitor entered the museum. I hurried down the hall, slid into the chair behind the desk, and looked toward the entrance.

Danny stood inside the front door. "Libby. I'm closing the shop for a while. I wanted to bring you your pearls before I left town."

Goosebumps sprang up on my arms. The words, by themselves, weren't threatening. But there was a hardness in his eyes that hadn't been there when I dropped off my pearls.

Danny walked toward the desk. With each step, his dress shoes made a sharp *ca-clack* on the hardwood floor.

Sam said something over the phone about the town birthday party, but it didn't quite register.

If Danny was leaving Dogwood Springs, it was probably because he knew someone suspected him of being the murderer.

Me.

For a split second, my mind went completely blank. But then I had an idea. "Ah, Sam, we'll have to talk later. I'm— I'm afraid you're right. I may have to meet with Ivy Whitfield. Very soon. I don't think I have a choice."

Danny laid a messenger bag on the desk and pulled out a small brown envelope. He opened it and poured my pearls into the palm of his hand. "Why don't you get off the phone, so you can see how nicely these turned out? Maybe try them on?" He stroked his mustache.

The action, which once had seemed vain, now reminded me of a villain in a silent movie. He'd killed Sheila. He'd killed Carl. And now... The image of Danny strangling me with those pearls flashed before my eyes. *Please, Sam, please, figure out what I'm saying.*

"Libby?" Sam sounded confused. "Meet with Ivy Whitfield? But she's dead..." Then he spoke more rapidly. "Are you in danger?"

"Yes, yes, I am." I tried to sound normal so I wouldn't tip off Danny.

Sam drew in a sharp breath. "I'm—"

But I didn't hear the rest.

Danny leaned forward, yanked the phone from my hand, and hung up.

"Really, Libby. You need to see the workmanship on this clasp." He spoke calmly, as if we were in his shop, as if he hadn't just grabbed my phone, tapped it to end my call, and set it on the desk. He rested back on his heels, then shifted the pearls and raised the clasp to where I couldn't help but see it. "Look how nice that is. You'd never know I added a small bit of gold to strengthen it."

"It's... It's lovely. Thank you so much for bringing me my pearls." I stood up, pretending to admire them but actually thinking about how I could escape. The desk was angled so that one corner to my right was against the wall of the entryway. To my left, though, I could slip out into the hall.

"Put them on," he said. "There's nothing I like better than seeing a satisfied customer, and I don't want to leave any loose ends when I drive out of town."

Loose ends. I didn't like the sound of that.

Suddenly, he moved to the side of the desk near the hall, pushing the pearls toward me and leaving me no way to escape.

I reached out a shaking hand and took the necklace. After a couple of attempts, I managed to fasten the clasp behind my neck, all the while scanning the shelves under the desk, searching for a weapon.

There was nothing, nothing of use. Brochures. The little plastic device that could read credit cards. Maps of the town given out by the Chamber of Commerce.

But what about the box of supplies for the games Imani and I had played with the kids from the community center? Could I do something with a jump rope? No, I'd probably just be handing Danny something else he could use to strangle me.

Why didn't we keep a Civil War sword at the front desk?

"Now, isn't that nice? Pearls are always so classy." He reached across the desk and gripped my arm with one hand. "Of course, they won't look quite as attractive after I kill you, but that's the price you have to pay."

My blood went cold. I tried to wrench my arm away but couldn't.

He let out an impatient snort. "I thought that when I stole those letters, it would teach you to stop sticking your nose into my business, but apparently not."

"But how... How did you learn about the letters?"

He gave me a look like I was a dim-witted child. "Because I heard you telling your dog about them over the microphone I hid in your fireplace."

"You hid a bug in my fireplace?"

"A couple of weeks ago. After you first stopped by the jewelry store. I knew exactly what you were up to. I'd read in the paper about how you solved that other murder, and truly, the clasp on your necklace wasn't that bad, and before I pointed it out, you didn't realize the pearls needed to be restrung. You only brought them in so you could pump me for information about the murder."

"So you broke into my apartment twice?" My words came out with a squeak. "Once to plant a bug and again later when you stole the letters?"

He gave an exaggerated shrug. "Breaking in wasn't hard. Picking locks is delicate work, but so is jewelry repair."

"But if you did it to send me a message, why did you take my laptop and TV?"

"Because I wanted you to get the message, not the cops. I figured if I stole a couple of other things, they were so stupid they'd think it was the burglar from downtown."

I shoved my shoulders back, hoping to look brave, and

tried to keep my voice from shaking. "You know you won't get away with killing me."

"I will." He gave me another look like he thought I was stupid. "No one but you really suspects me."

"Leaving town won't look suspicious?"

"I'm a pretty smooth talker. I had to be to make a living selling to the tourist crowd. After I'm somewhere far, far away, I'll put out the word that losing my great-aunt made me realize how short life is. And with no family left here in town, I decided to follow my lifelong dream and move to someplace tropical."

"But everyone will know you killed me. I've told people, even shown people, the letters."

He rolled his eyes. "You're lying. You told your dog. That was all."

"No, I—" Wait. If the only conversations that he'd heard had been the ones I had in my apartment, that was probably all he knew. I had been in my apartment when I called the police this morning to make an appointment to see Detective Harper, but I'd talked with Sam here at the museum and the rest of my friends at Alice's. When I'd told the police my suspicions about Danny and the letters, we were outside. So for all Danny knew, I was lying, and I hadn't told anyone yet. And that was probably what he subconsciously wanted to believe.

He tightened his grip on my arm. "I've been listening outside. That other woman said she'd be back before four. You're just telling me a bunch of lies to try to keep me here until she returns." He jerked my arm and then reached his other hand into his messenger bag and drew out a long knife.

Light from the overhead fixture glinted off the blade.

I gasped for breath, my heartbeat pounding inside my head. "No, really—"

"Time's up, Libby. Don't worry, it will be quick." He raised the knife above me, ready to plunge it into my chest.

Chapter Twenty-Six

MY HEART RACED SO FAST that it felt like it was about to explode, but I held up a trembling hand. "Hold on! You need to read some of the texts on my phone." Surely, Danny had to realize he was beaten if he saw the photo of the will.

Doubt flashed through his eyes, but he glanced at my phone on the desk and lowered the knife a few inches.

I picked up my phone and opened the text messages, scrolling through them slowly and deliberately, as if I was searching for one that was hard to find, instead of the most recent one from Cleo, the photo of the will. "Here." I stretched my arm out as far to the right as I could, placing the phone so that he'd either have to move back to the middle of the other side of the desk to see it or let go of me or the knife to pick it up.

He kept his grip tightly on the knife and on my arm but moved right to look at the phone. His lips tightened. "Not that blasted will that Sheila said she found." He leaned down to see more clearly and, ever so slightly, loosened his grip on my arm.

I twisted away, slipping free, and I grabbed the bag of marbles from below the desk.

He jabbed the knife toward me, but I raced down the hall toward the back door, pouring hundreds of marbles behind me onto the hardwood floor.

"You little—" He let out a scream.

I glanced back.

He was flailing, his feet rolling on marbles. A half second later, he fell flat on his back as the front door burst open.

"Freeze," Officer Tate yelled and pointed his gun at Danny.

An officer I didn't know waded his way through the marbles, shuffling his feet along the ground to avoid stepping on them. He grabbed Danny, pinned his arms behind his back, and cuffed him.

I exhaled loudly and sank to my knees with my back against the wall.

"Are you all right, ma'am?" Officer Tate holstered his weapon and carefully moved toward me.

"I am." Tears welled in my eyes. "I just ... almost wasn't."

"Sam Collins called and said you were in danger. And Adelaide Murphy had just called the chief and said she thought Danny might be the killer. When we saw Danny's car with its personalized plates outside, we pulled right up on the curb and ran in. I'm afraid we may have done a number on the grass in front of the museum."

"I couldn't care less." I'd be more than happy to replant the grass out front. All I cared about was the fact that I was alive. "Thank you. Thank you both."

Detective Harper appeared at my side. "Libby, are you injured?"

"No. I'm all right." I brushed my tears away.

"What happened?"

I told him the whole story. Well, most of the story. I may have left out the fact that I interviewed several people I considered suspects. But I told him that Danny had admitted to killing both Sheila and Carl and all about the handwritten will that Sheila had found. And I explained that it had been Danny, not the downtown burglar, who broke into my apartment.

"But why did Danny come after you? You weren't snooping, were you? Not after I told you not to?"

"I had talked with Danny a long time before you said that. How was I to know that he'd broken in and planted a bug in my fireplace? And heard that I'd found letters from Marjorie's lover in a purse I bought at the auction and figured out that he was the killer?"

"That's all well and good, but from now on, if anything suspicious happens in Dogwood Springs, you are to stay—"

"Oh my gosh." I raised a hand to cover my mouth.

"What?"

"I just figured out why Bella kept barking at my fireplace. I thought there was a squirrel up there. She absolutely hates squirrels. But it was the bug. I think she knew it was there."

Anyone else might think I was crazy, but if there was one thing Detective Harper and I agreed on, it was the fact that Bella was smart.

He raised one eyebrow. "Does the timing fit? She started barking after you first talked to Danny?"

"The very next day. I bet he planted the bug that evening when I took Bella out to the park."

He ran a hand over his chin. "Well, that is one smart dog. I'll send someone over to find the bug and remove it. I'd be interested to know if your 'squirrel problem' suddenly goes away."

"I bet it does. I just bet it does." I shook my head. Would Bella ever stop surprising me?

Officer Tate opened the door and leaned in. "Sir? Whenever you're done, there's a woman out here who works at the museum and wants to see Miss Ballard."

The detective angled his head toward the door. "Why don't you go out and speak to her, and then we can go down to the station, where I can get a formal statement."

"Thank you." I went outside and was immediately enveloped in a hug from Imani.

"Are you okay?" She stepped back and looked at me.

"I am."

"Thank God." She gestured to the front lawn of the museum. "When I got back from dropping those three boxes off at the schools, I saw that police cruiser, and then they wouldn't let me in because they said it was a crime scene..." She let out a heavy sigh and hugged me again.

"It was definitely more excitement than I was expecting this afternoon," I said. "But I think everything is okay now. The police have arrested Danny Larsen. You know, the jeweler from downtown?"

Her eyes grew wide.

Behind her, a blue Tesla drove by.

A minute later, as I was explaining what Danny had done, Sam ran around the side of the building.

"Libby!" His shoulders sagged. "You're all right."

Imani looked at me, then at Sam, and slowly dipped her chin. She took my hand, squeezed it, and edged away. "We'll talk more tomorrow."

Sam closed the distance between us in less than a second and drew me into a hug.

My throat thickened, and I pulled him closer.

"I was so worried about you," he said in a low voice.

For a moment, I stayed there, wrapped in his arms. Then I stepped back and looked up at him. "Thank you. If I hadn't been on the phone with you, and if you hadn't understood what I meant and called the cops..."

He shook his head. "Saying you were going to meet with a dead woman was a rather strong indicator that something was wrong. Did he hurt you?"

"No. I'm fine. Just a little wobbly."

He slid a hand under my elbow. "Are you free to go?"

"I need to go to the police station and give an official statement."

"Well, can I pick you up when you're done to drive you home? I could take your keys and move your car to your apartment and then walk back here to my car."

I let out my breath with a *whoosh*. After being attacked, the idea of having someone with me, someone I trusted, sounded really, really good. "That would be wonderful." I gave Sam my keys and headed to the station with Detective Harper.

Chapter Twenty-Seven

BY THE TIME I'd finished at the police station, Cleo, Alice, and Zeke had heard what happened. Detective Harper had sent an officer over to my apartment, and, with my permission, Sam had let him in so he could remove the bug and dust for prints around the fireplace.

When I walked out of the station shortly before six, Sam was parked right in front.

I climbed into his car and sank into the seat.

Bella stuck her head between the seats.

"Bella!" I'd been so shaken that I hadn't even noticed her in the back.

"She wanted to come," Sam said. "Having the police in the apartment got her worked up. And when I asked if she wanted to see you, she went right to the door."

"But your car..." Doggie toenails couldn't be good for his upholstery.

"I had a stadium blanket in my trunk."

Bella licked my cheek.

"Hey, sweetie." I petted her head and looked her in the eyes. "I'm so sorry I didn't understand. You tried to tell me —and every person who came into my apartment—about the bug. But we just didn't get it. I thought you were upset about a squirrel, and all the while, you were trying to keep me safe."

She gave a loud woof, which I took as a yes, and I told Sam about how Danny had planted the bug in my fireplace.

He turned to her. "Quite the smart cookie, aren't you, Bella? I'm not surprised. Dogs are amazing." He looked back at me. "The police say it's going to be a while before they're done. Cleo wondered if you'd like to meet her, Alice, and someone named Zeke at the café for dinner. They're desperate to hear all the details of what happened."

"The café sounds great." Just thinking about their food made me hungry.

Despite the tourists, Sam was able to get a spot only a couple of blocks down Main Street from the café, and Alice sat at our favorite table, the one in the corner of the outdoor dining area with a shady spot near the fence for Bella.

Sam, Bella, and I made our way over, and Alice pulled me into a hug. "I'm so glad you're okay."

Then Zeke and Cleo arrived together. I introduced them both to Sam and, after Cleo had hugged me, we all sat down. Zeke seemed a little starstruck by Sam but eagerly sat beside him. I sat between Sam and Cleo, who wanted to know everything immediately.

"Let's order first," I said. "It's quite a story, especially with what Danny told Detective Harper."

While we waited for the server to come to our table, Sam and Zeke began discussing something related to computers called Linux. I didn't know what it was, but Zeke's eyes shone, and his nervousness around Sam disappeared.

Five minutes later, a server had brought our drinks and taken our orders.

I drew in a deep breath and then explained what I'd been able to piece together, using what the detective told me. While her husband was still alive, Marjorie had made her original will, leaving everything to her husband, and if he died before her, to Danny and her other great-nephew.

"That makes sense," Alice said. "She wouldn't want to mention her illegitimate child in front of her husband."

I nodded. "So, years later, after her husband died, she learned she had a fast-moving cancer. A couple of days later, she made an appointment with her lawyer, but he was out of town for two weeks, so in the meantime, she wrote her new will by hand."

"And that's the will that Sheila found," Cleo said. "The one that left everything to Lisa."

Alice's nose wrinkled. "Why didn't Marjorie contact Lisa years earlier, after her husband died?"

"I bet we'll never know for sure," Cleo said. "But maybe she thought that if Lisa had been raised thinking her mother had died, she wouldn't welcome Marjorie into her life. Maybe Marjorie was afraid of being rejected."

Alice pressed her lips together and sighed. "That does make sense, but it sure is sad."

"It is. And so is the way she died," I said. "Everyone thought Marjorie died of natural causes, but when the detective interrogated Danny, he admitted that he killed her. He said she'd told him of her cancer, and he wanted to reduce her suffering, but apparently, he'd made a number of risky investments and was about to lose everything, including his house. He managed to piece things together to buy himself some time, but he needed the money from the inheritance as soon as possible, so he smothered her."

"Why didn't anyone notice she'd been murdered?" Zeke asked.

"I guess they just assumed it was a natural death because she was elderly and had such an aggressive form of cancer." I took a sip of my iced tea.

Cleo leaned in. "Did you learn how Danny knew that Sheila had found the will?"

"Detective Harper thinks she found it the previous night, after we saw her, and, after she texted Adelaide, she took it to the auction house and put it in the safe."

"So, why would he kill her?" Zeke said. "The proof was locked up."

I shook my head. "Danny said he saw her the next morning, and when he made a joke and told her that she'd better make sure the day was profitable, she told him not to count his chickens before they hatched." I rolled my eyes. "I bet that 'joke' didn't sound funny at all. When I heard him talking to Jeannie that day, he sounded desperate for money."

"Uh-oh." Cleo ran a hand over her collarbone. "Sheila didn't like to be bossed around. I bet she told him she'd found the will."

"She did. But Danny thought Sheila had just found it that morning and that it was one of the papers she had on her clipboard. He killed her, then searched the papers and her pockets but couldn't find it. The rest of the morning, until the body was found, he continued to sneak around Marjorie's house searching for the will."

"So, at that point, he not only had financial trouble, but he'd also committed murder. Not good," Sam said. "Not good at all."

"And then he broke into her house, trying to find the will, but it wasn't there." Cleo pressed her lips into a fine line. "Which explains why he trashed the place."

"When I questioned him at the jewelry store, he got even more nervous, and he planted a bug in my apartment to see what I knew. Bella tried to tell me it was there, but I didn't get it." I rubbed her ears. "Then Danny apparently tried to break into the auction house but couldn't. A few days later, Carl Wilson found the will and tried to get Danny to pay him to keep silent."

"Blackmail." Zeke let out a low whistle. "That didn't work out very well for Mr. Wilson."

"And if Jeannie knew about the money Carl was skimming," I added, "even if she knew Carl had been blackmailing Danny, she couldn't tell the cops without making her husband look bad and possibly ending up arrested herself."

Sam's forehead wrinkled. "Who's Jeannie?"

Cleo explained. "For a while, we thought she had to be the killer."

"And we suspected Sandy, who owns the gift shop on Main Street," Alice said. "But she was innocent, although I heard she has her own problems."

"Oh?" I took a quick drink of my tea. "People already know about her son's drug use?"

"Not only that." Alice leaned in. "Her son was the one committing all the burglaries downtown. He started out stealing to pay for his drug habit but moved on to making bigger and bigger thefts."

"Wow," Zeke said. "He may go straight from rehab into prison."

"It seems likely," Alice said.

"Sandy's son was breaking into stores downtown. Carl Wilson was skimming money from each of his auction clients. And Danny Larsen killed three people to get his hands on Marjorie Billington's money." Sam sat back from the table and slowly shook his head. "I see a whole different side of Dogwood Springs when I'm with you guys."

I shrugged. "At least the police no longer suspect Cleo of killing Carl." I patted her shoulder.

"Thanks to you, Libby." She looked over at me, her eyes shining. "I can't tell you how much it means to me that Sheila's killer has been caught. We're having a memorial service for her in a couple of weeks and burying her ashes in the family plot in the cemetery. I'm so glad we can lay her to rest with a sense of closure."

I leaned over and hugged her. "It was the least I could do. You're my best friend."

She hugged me back and pulled out her phone to show us photos of the silk flower arrangement she'd created for the gravesite. "It took me several tries to get it right, but I finally got all the crystals hot-glued onto the flowers the way I wanted. Plain silk flowers wouldn't be bright enough for Sheila, even if they were red. She'd want a little bling."

"They're perfect," Alice said.

Zeke agreed. "She'd like those a lot."

"I can't believe Danny almost killed you too, Libby," Alice said.

I shuddered. "Things did get a little sticky there at the end, but if we hadn't investigated, and I hadn't bought Lot 7 at the auction, I think Danny might have gotten away with it."

"I'm just glad you're safe." Sam grabbed my hand under the table and gave it a quick squeeze.

He gazed at me until Bella nosed in between us, and he turned his attention to her.

While Sam was looking down at Bella, Cleo and Alice's eyes met. They both grinned.

I had a feeling I was going to get a few comments about that look Sam gave me.

In spite of the ribbing I knew I'd get, I was grateful for my friends. I looked around the table at each of them, and my heart filled. "I'm really lucky to have you guys." To help me with my sleuthing and to round out my world. I still had my family back in Ohio, but Cleo, Alice, Zeke, and Bella had become my family here in Dogwood Springs. They were there for me when I needed them, and I could count on them.

And Sam...

Well, who knew what would happen between me and Sam?

Epilogue

Saturday, Sept. 16

I STEPPED into the hall and locked my office. For a second, I stood staring at the sign on the door that said "Libby Ballard, Museum Director."

Then I headed down the main staircase of the Dogwood Springs History Museum, into noise and chaos.

Noise and chaos and success.

It was only the middle of the afternoon, but we'd already reached more than three hundred visitors at the town birthday party. I'd refilled the toilet paper twice in the women's bathrooms—one of the less glamorous jobs of a museum director. And we'd run out of the flyers about our fall programming, so I'd dashed upstairs to print some off from my computer. They were only black and white, not color like the ones Imani had printed at the shop, but they would still help promote our events.

"I'm back." Alice walked in from the hall that led to the conference room and met me at the base of the front stairs. "I bought eight extra sheet cakes at the grocery store and stashed them in the fridge. They aren't specially decorated, but at least it's cake. The cake I made is only going to serve two hundred, even if we cut the pieces small." She waved a hand toward the crowd around us and to the area outside the front windows, where Imani was leading a large group of children in a game of Mother, May I. "I can't believe the turnout."

"I can't either. Thank you for all you've done."

"It was a group effort," she said. "The board pitched in, but you and Imani and Rodney did most of it. And the weather..."

"Indeed." We'd gotten so lucky. The humidity was low, the high about eighty—a perfect September day.

I moved out of the way, allowing a group to enter the display room with the new exhibit about the founder of the town.

Rodney, back at work after his knee replacement, had done a fabulous job, and had been thrilled when Lisa Brown donated the armoire that Jedidiah Siler and his wife, Frances, brought with them from New York State.

I'd talked with Lisa and, though she had been shocked to learn that her father had lied to her about her mom, she knew he'd done it out of love, probably even moving to the town where she grew up to protect her from any questions. "I'm sure my dad and Marjorie each did the best they could at the time. I can't judge them or see it as a reflection on me," she said.

A healthy way to view it, in my opinion. But still, it was a pity Marjorie never got to meet her daughter.

I looked toward the room with the armoire for a moment, then pulled my mind back to the birthday party.

Cleo waved from the back of the group going in to see the new exhibit.

Outside, Zeke laughed with a girl his age.

And the other board members wandered the crowd, all appearing very pleased with the event.

Plus, Sam had stopped by earlier, wished me good luck, and promised to take me out to dinner once I survived the afternoon.

The museum even had the painting he had found in his attic, the original Clayton Smithton, on display. An art professor from the university had volunteered her time for the event and was delightedly showing visitors the new piece and explaining how one girl in the portrait, who we now knew was Ivy Whitfield, had been painted out.

I'd considered doing research to learn more about Ivy and her family before we unveiled the painting but decided it might be good for attendance to release the information to the public bit by bit, giving people a reason to return to the museum as we learned more about the painting. And, what with getting ready for the town birthday party, I'd been a little busy.

The boxes I bought at the auction had indeed contained treasure—the letters Tobias had written to Marjorie, which the police had found at Danny's house and I'd given to Lisa Brown, and the vintage purses. I'd kept one Chanel bag. It was too small for my everyday use, but it would be great for formal events. It was by far the most expensive item in my wardrobe, but I decided that if you found a treasure, you ought to keep part of it. Some of the other purses I donated to the museum. We could use them in a display on fashion through the ages. The rest I'd sold for a tidy profit, which I used to replenish my savings, which had taken a double hit with the divorce and the move.

All in all, my $30 gamble had paid off well.

Plus, Detective Harper had recovered my emerald earrings and my pearl ring from Danny's home.

And what a difference the past few weeks had made. Now I knew I could make a go of my position as director of the Dogwood Springs History Museum.

Rodney, Imani, and I had gelled into a solid team. I had begun to make connections in the community, regularly meeting with local service organizations and potential donors. And people once again viewed the museum as a vital part of the town, a place they and their children could visit to learn more about their history in an engaging and entertaining way. What's more, largely thanks to Sam's donation of the Clayton Smithton painting, they saw it as a top attraction to recommend to tourists.

I now stood on firm ground, no longer worried about failure. The confidence was energizing, and the possibilities for the museum seemed limitless. More than one person had told me that they'd come only to see Alice's cake and been surprised to see how much they enjoyed learning about the history of the area. One woman even told me she planned to send her friends. Talk about warming my history-loving heart.

I couldn't wait for our next big event.

But first, we had cake to serve.

Once Alice was ready, I opened the window near a display about the first school in the area, the same school Ivy Whitfield had attended, and I rang the old school bell. Then I called the crowd together near a table on the front lawn, and Alice unveiled her creation—an enormous cake designed to look just like the museum with its tall white columns and twin chimneys.

The crowd cheered.

My heart swelled with pride. I gazed out at a wonderful mix of all kinds of people and thought about what the museum offered the town. Everyone was welcome. Everyone's involvement mattered. Everyone had access to learn more about the history of Dogwood Springs, to see things that might let them understand both the past and the present in a new light.

And I got to be a part of it.

"Thank you, Alice. The cake is fabulous." I hugged her.

She beamed and brushed aside the praise, saying she'd had fun making it.

And we began serving.

Finally, at five thirty, half an hour after the town birthday party had been scheduled to end, Imani, Rodney, and I managed to usher the last guests out of the museum.

An hour later, after we'd counted the donations and put the place mostly back to rights, I texted Sam as he'd requested, to let him know I was headed home.

I'd driven in for the event, even though it was only a few blocks. I'd been in the museum business long enough to know that after the crowd left an event, the day would start to catch up with me.

Once I arrived home, Bella galloped to the back door to meet me. I patted her head, told her what a good girl she was, and let her out for a few minutes. I fixed her dinner and, while she ate, I clipped my hair up and took a quick shower. Then I dressed and redid my makeup. I was putting on earrings when my doorbell rang.

I opened the door to the entryway, then the main door, and found Sam on the front porch, holding a large picnic basket.

Bella wriggled outside and rubbed her head against his leg.

Sam shifted the basket to the other side of his body and petted her. "Did things continue to go well at the birthday party?"

I waved him inside. "They did. It was amazing. We had more than five hundred people visit today."

"Wow! That's incredible!" He held up the basket. "I thought you might have had enough of crowds for the day.

We can eat here, or, if you'd like, we could drive out to Dogwood Springs Park and picnic there."

"Ooh! The park sounds heavenly. Can Bella come too? I've been so busy the past twenty-four hours that I feel like I've neglected her."

"Bella is most definitely invited."

I changed my shoes, filled a container with water for Bella, and packed a water bowl, her Frisbee, and—since she'd finished her dinner—a couple of dog biscuits.

By the time I'd answered all of Sam's questions about the day, excitedly sharing some of the kind comments visitors had made, we reached the park. He followed the park road until we spotted an empty picnic table under a big oak with a lovely view of the stream fed by the spring. Cicadas hummed, the air was tinged with a hint of the mossy scent of the stream, and a gentle breeze wafted by from time to time. A perfect evening.

As we unpacked the car, Sam pointed in the bag where I'd packed Bella's gear. His eyes lit. "Is that Bella's Frisbee?"

"Those aren't my tooth marks." I chuckled.

"Would you mind if I..." He picked up the Frisbee and looked at me, his face as excited as a little boy's.

"Go ahead," I said. "I'll unpack the picnic."

Sam carried the basket to the table, helped me spread out a checkered cloth, and then headed off to play with Bella.

Meanwhile, I opened the basket, which Sam said he'd bought from the café, fully packed with everything we'd need, including the tablecloth. I found cold fried chicken, potato salad made with tiny, halved red-skin potatoes, a fruit salad, some of the café's excellent coleslaw, a thermos of iced tea, and an enormous serving of gooey butter cake.

My mouth was already watering.

I poured Bella's water and set out the two doggie biscuits I'd packed for her dessert.

A few minutes later, Sam and Bella ran toward me. Bella gulped some water and flopped down on the concrete pad beneath the picnic table, crunching loudly on a treat.

Sam washed his hands at a nearby spigot and wiped them on his jeans. "Good enough." He held them up and grinned.

"The food looks delicious," I said. "Thank you."

"My pleasure." He gestured for me to help myself, and the two of us loaded our plates.

I gladly began. The food tasted even better than it looked.

After a few minutes, Sam set down his fork. "Hey, I have news."

A tingle of excitement ran down my spine. "Oh?"

"I found out something about Ivy this afternoon."

My mouth was full of fried chicken, but I motioned for him to tell me.

"I went on that website you mentioned, and I searched the census records for Silersville." He pushed a bite of slaw back and forth on his plate. "I hope you don't mind that I took a look without you. After I saw the painting up at the museum, I really wanted to know more."

"I don't mind at all." It was precisely the reaction I'd

hoped to create with the display. And I wasn't going to mention it, but it seemed like Sam might have been bitten by the history bug.

"I found Ivy listed as living here with her parents, Horace and Blanche Whitfield, as well as a younger sister, Florence Whitfield, in 1900. Ivy was thirteen, and her younger sister was nine."

"Good job! So now we know the names of everyone in the painting. I'm sure we can learn more about what happened to Ivy if we keep digging. There are a lot of clues if you know where to look." I scooped some slaw onto my plastic fork.

"I'd love to investigate the painting with you. It seems like a good reason to see you a lot more often." He looked over at me, and his gaze held mine. "You're something special, Libby Ballard."

My chest tightened. *Something special.* The same words my ex had used. How could I hear them and not be slammed with insecurity and fear?

But how fair was it to judge Sam based on my ex-husband? My ex may have been a jerk, but Sam wasn't.

Sam was the man who had arranged this lovely picnic. The man who had set up the catered dinner so I could be the first to see the display about my great-great grand-mother. And the man who had figured out what I meant when I was in danger and mentioned Ivy Whitfield.

Plus, I'd seen from Marjorie what could happen if you waited too long, if you didn't embrace all life offered. She could have reached out to her daughter after her husband died. Instead, she never met her only child. Any opportunity they had for a relationship had been lost.

It was time for me to trust a bit more. To take another small step in building a life here in Dogwood Springs.

A life made fuller by Bella, by my colleagues at the museum, Imani and Rodney, by my friends Cleo, Alice, and Zeke.

And by Sam.

I looked into his eyes, and the tension in my chest eased. My heart filled with hope, and I leaned across the table and took his hand. "I'd love to learn more about Ivy. And I'd love to see you more often, Sam."

⁓

Thank you for reading this book!

Are you ready to return to Dogwood Springs for another cozy mystery? Join Libby, Bella, and their friends in the next book in the series, HOME TOURS, HISTORY & HOMICIDE.

Event-Planning Tip No. 57: Avoid any connection between your fundraiser and murder.

Libby Ballard, director of the history museum in the small town of Dogwood Springs, Missouri, is excited to be organizing a tour of historic homes to raise funds for the museum. With plans in full swing, she drops by to confirm details with one of the homeowners and makes a gruesome discovery—the homeowner has been murdered.

Who could have possibly wanted to kill a local doctor, and why?

The police suspect the victim's wife, but Libby thinks there's more to the story. With the historic homes tour in jeopardy and violence escalating, Libby, her friends, and her trusty golden retriever dig deeper into the case.

But will Libby be able to uncover the killer's identity before they strike again?

Don't miss this thrilling tale of mystery, murder, and small-town secrets!

If you like a cozy mystery with a pet who will win your heart, friends who feel like family, and a hint of romance, you'll love HOME TOURS, HISTORY & HOMICIDE.

Don't miss your free reader bonuses! Join Sally's cozy mystery newsletter to:

- download the prequel to the Dogwood Springs series, BED & BREAKFAST & BURGLARY, which is available only to newsletter subscribers
- read exclusive bonus content for every book, such as a scene in Bella's point of view
- learn about new releases, and more!

Visit Sally's website at www.sallybayless.com/free-mystery/ to join.

See all the books in the Dogwood Springs Cozy Mystery Series at www.sallybayless.com.

Acknowledgments

When I think of all the people who helped me with this book, I am truly overwhelmed. I cannot imagine writing without such amazing support.

First, I want to send a big thank you to the cozy mystery community. Since I released the first book in this series, I've been delighted by the encouragement I've received from readers and fellow authors alike. What a joy to be a part of this world!

A special thank you to my critique partners, Susan Anne Mason and Tammy Doherty, who once again shared their storytelling skills and knowledge of the craft of writing to make this book better. I appreciate you so much!

Thank you to my accountability partner, Cathryn Brown, for her encouragement and for helping me keep on top of my publishing business.

My beta readers are phenomenal. They offered so many suggestions that made this book a more enjoyable read. Thanks to Debbie Edwards, Ken Edwards, Barbara Hackel, Janice Huwe, Martha Long, Kim Mather, Carrie Saunders, and Stephanie Smith. You guys are great!

Paula Lester of Polaris Editing edited this book and helped make it shine. Thank you, Paula!

Donna Lynn Rogers of DLR Cover Designs created the wonderful cover. Donna, I'm so grateful to have you designing my covers. I love them!

Finally, I want to thank my family—my husband, Dave, and our two grown children, Michael and Laurel, for their encouragement and patience. A special thank you to Laurel, who also beta read this book.

If, in spite of the assistance from all of these people, errors slipped in, please know that the mistakes were mine alone.

About the Author

After many years away, Sally Bayless lives in her hometown in the Missouri Ozarks. She's married and has two grown children. When not working on her next book, she enjoys reading, BBC mysteries, word puzzles, swimming, and shopping for cute shoes.

www.ingramcontent.com/pod-product-compliance
Lightning Source LLC
Chambersburg PA
CBHW050845190726
48286CB00007B/2236